Capital Tales

CAPITAL TALES

BRIAN FAWCETT

CAPITAL. — CAPITAL.

Capital (kæ·pităl), *sb.*[1] Forms: 3 **capitale**, 5 **capital**, 6–7 **capitell, -el**, (7 **capitull, -ol**), 7– **capital**. [Answers to L. *capitell-um* in same sense (dim. of *caput* head, or rather of its dim. *capitulum*), and its representatives, It. *capitello*, OF. *capitel*, *chapitel*, now *chapiteau*; but from the beginning tending to confusion with the adj. CAPITAL, to which it is now assimilated. Italian influence favoured *capitel l* in the 17th c.]

1. The head or top of a column or pillar.

c 1250 *Land Cokaygne* 69 in *E. E. P.* (1862) 158 Þe pilers.. Wiþ harlas, and capitale Of grene jaspe and rede corale. 1413 LYDG. *Pylgr. Sowle* IV. xxxvi. (1483) 83 The legges ben as it were pylers.. the knees ben the capitals and the feete the bases. 1563 SHUTE *Archit.* B j b, In the Capitel, was set Voluta.. for an ornature and garnishment of the Capitell. 1604 DRAYTON *Owle* 629 From the Base, up to the Capitell. 1660 BLOOME *Archit.* E a, Corinthian Capitall. 1670 LASSELS *Voy. Italy* II. 157 Four great Pillars.. adorned with Capitels.. of brasse guilt. 1747 *Scheme Equip. Men of War* 60 On the Capitol, Victory, Trade, Peace and Plenty might be expressed. 1851 RUSKIN *Stones Ven.* (1874) I. vii. 72 A capital is only the cornice of a column.

2. The head or cap of a chimney, crucible, etc.

1715 DESAGULIERS *Fires Impr.* 79 Such a Capital will wholly hinder the Wind from going into the Chimney. 1753 CHAMBERS *Cycl. Supp.* s. v., Capital of a lanthorn.. Capital of a mill. 1800 HENRY *Epit. Chem.* (1808) 148 An alembic, covered with its capital.

¶ **3.** A chapter of a book. (for CAPITLE.)

1819 SCOTT *Ivanhoe* xxxvii, Holy St. Bernard in the rule of our.. profession, hath said, in the fifty-ninth capital, etc.

Capital, *sb.*[2]: see B. under the adj.

Capital (kæ·pităl), *a.* and *sb.*[2] Forms: 3–4 **capitale**, 5–7 **capitall e**, 5–6 **capytal**(l, 7 **capitoll**, 4– **capital**. [a. F. *capital* (12th c.), ad. L. *capitāl-is*, in legal and ecclesiastical use. The actual F. descendant of the L. word is *cheptel* (pronounced *chetel*).]

A. *adj.* **I.** Relating to the head.

†**1.** Of or pertaining to the head or top. *Obs.*

a 1225 *Ancr. R.* 238 Wiðuten eddren capitalen þet bledden on his hefde. 1486 *Bk. St. Albans, Her.* F j, Sparris.. put.. by the maner of an hede, and ij syche sparris ionyt togedyr make a capitall sygne. 1616 CHAPMAN *Homer's Batrachom.* 9 Their parts capitall They hid. 1667 MILTON *P. L.* XII. 383 His [the Serpent's] capital bruise. 1688 R. HOLME *Armoury* III. xiii. 34 A Pillar Composed in the Capital part.

2. Affecting, or involving loss of, the head or life.

1483 CAXTON *Gold. Leg.* 184/3 To haue capytal sentence & be beheded. 1581 LAMBARDE *Eiren.* I. xii. (1588) 67 Capitall (or deadly) punishment is done sundry wayes. 1770 LANGHORNE *Plutarch* (1879) I. 181/2 Cimon.. narrowly escaped a capital sentence. 1880 *Spectator* 19 Dec. 1487 We never remember a capital verdict upon such insufficient evidence.

b Punishable by death.

1526 FRITH *Purgat.* 201 Whosoever hath committed a capital crime. 1660 STRADLING *Serm.* (1692) 168 The Egyptians made it Capital to affirm that their God Apis was dead. *a* 1745 SWIFT *Wks.* (1841) II. 154 Guilty of a capital crime. 1827 HALLAM *Const. Hist.* (1876) III. xvii. 330 It was capital to preach even in houses.

†**c.** Of persons: Dealing with capital crimes; also, capitally condemned. *Obs.*

1583 STUBBES *Anat. Abus.* II. 106 They, as Capytall Iudges, geue definytiue sentence of lyfe and death. 1631 GOUGE *God's Arrowes* III. § 60. 295 Putting capitall malefactors to death. 1644 PRYNNE *Check to Britan.* 4 An impenitent, obdurate, Capitall Delinquent.

†**d.** Fatal. *Obs.*

a 1626 BACON (J.) War, which is capital to thousands. 1702 COLLIER *M. Antoninus* 11 In the Reign of Adrian an excellency of almost any kind was sometimes Capital to the Owner.

e. *Roman Law.* Involving loss of civil rights.

1838 ARNOLD *Hist. Rome* (1846) I. xiv. 289 The punishment of a libeller involved in it a *diminutio capitis*, and was thus in the Roman sense of the term capital.

†**3.** Said of an enemy or enmity: Deadly, mortal. *Obs.*

1375 BARBOUR *Bruce* III. 2 The lord off lorne.. That wes capitale ennymy To the king. 1500 ARNOLDE *Chron.* (1811) 283 A capital enmyte lyke to haue endured for euer. 1670 COTTON *Espernon* I. III. 109 The Bishop was his capital Enemy. 1760 HUME *Hist. Eng.* (1806) IV. liv. 162 The capital enemy of their country.

4. *fig.* Of defects, errors, and the like: Fatal, vitally injurious, most serious, radical. (Passing into sense 6 d.)

1538 STARKEY *England* 128 You have notyd such [faults] as be most capytal. 1581 MULCASTER *Positions* xxxiii. (1887) 121 Immoderate exercise.. a very capitall enemie to health. 1618 T. TAYLOR *Comm. Titus* ii. 10 (1619) 429 It is more capitall to smite the master then a stranger. 1734 tr. *Rollin's Anc. Hist.* (1827) II. II. 34 Hannibal's stay at Capua was a capital blemish in his conduct. 1855 PRESCOTT *Philip II*, II. v. (1857) 249 In the outset, he seems to have fallen into a capital error.

II. Standing at the head. *lit.* and *fig.*

5. Of words and letters: † Standing at the head of a page, or at the beginning of a line or paragraph, initial (*obs.*). *Capital letters*: letters of the form and relative size used in this position.

c 1391 CHAUCER *Astrol.* 8 This same bordure is devyded.. with 23 lettres capitals. 1432–50 tr. *Higden* (Rolls Ser.) IV. 299 The capitalle letters.. expresse this sentence. 1490 CAXTON *Eneydos* xxii. 84 The grete capitalle lettres of the bygynnynge.. of the psalmes and chapytres.. ben alle mayde fayre. 1584 POWEL *Lloyd's Cambria* 9 It is easy for the C. Capitall to creepe in. 1660 PEPYS *Diary* 11 June, To have the capitall words wrote with red ink. 1676 MOXON *Print. Lett.* 10 Use a Capital Letter.. in all Proper Names. 1811 J. BANNATINE in *Monthly Mag.* XXXIV. 429 One very modern improvement in writing and printing.. dropping the capital letters, except in the beginning of sentences, etc.

6. Chief; head-: **a.** of persons. *arch.* or *Obs.*

c 1425 WYNTOUN *Cron.* VI. xix. 37 Of þis Lawch are thre capytale. 1461–83 *Liber Niger Edw. IV* in *Housch. Ord.* 73 This sergeaunt, capitall Buttler. 1530 *Test. Ebor.* (Surtees) V. 293 Capital Sanctes under God of the aforsaid kirkes. 1614 T. ADAMS *Divel's Banq.* 213 Diseases, which be Deaths capitall Chirurgions. 1683 *Lond. Gaz.* No. 1866/4 The Mayor, Aldermen, Bayliff, Capital Burgesses, and Commonalty of.. Waymouth. 1753 CHAMBERS *Cycl. Supp.*, *Capital lord*.. the lord of the fee. 1820 in *Risdon's Surv. Devon* 426 A Mayor, assisted by 18 capital burgesses.

b. of mansions, estates, towns, and cities. *Capital manor*: one held *in capite*, or directly from the King. *Capital messuage*: that occupied by the owner of a property containing several messuages. *Capital town* or *city* = CAPITAL *sb.* (see B. 2 below).

1539 *Act 31 Hen. VIII*, v, The saide manour of Hampton courte shall.. be the chiefe and capitall place and parte of the saide honour of Hampton courte. 1601 HOLLAND *Pliny* I. 125 From thence.. to the capitoll towne of the Arachosians, 515 miles. 1642 PERKINS *Prof. Bk.* v. § 406. 175 The heire is not compellable to assigne unto his mother.. the capitall messuage which was his Fathers. 1667 MILTON *P. L.* II. 924 Battering Engines bent to rase Som Capital City. *Ibid.* XI. 343 This had been Perhaps thy Capital Seate, from whence had spred All generations. 1768 BLACKSTONE *Comm.* II. 214 The eldest son had the capital fee or principal feud of his father's possessions. 1774 T. WARTON *Hist. Eng. Poetry* (1840) I. 18 Chained in the cloister, or church, of some capital monastery. 1809 BAWDEN tr. *Domesday Bk.* 589 The Abbot of Westminster claims all this because the capital manor is given to St. Peter.

†**c.** of ships: 'Of the line'; first-rate. *Obs.*

1688 *Lond. Gaz.* No. 2397/4 The Capital Ships are off of Torbay about 4 Leagues from the Shore. 1766 SMOLLETT *Hist. Eng.* (1804) V. 248 Of these capital ships (those of the line), 17 were stationed in the East Indies.

d. of other things.

a 1535 MORE *De quat. Noviss.* Wks. 85/2, Ii. capitall vyces, that is to wit enuye and couityce. 1597 J. PAYNE *Royal Exch.* 44 Love ys the capitall affection in men and wemen. 1671 MILTON *Samson* 394 To win from me My capital secret. 1749 CHESTERF. *Lett.* II. clxxxv. 189 The Last Supper, by Paul Veronese.. is reckoned his capital performance. 1872 R. W. DALE *Commandm.* 7 The old traditions.. made Obedience the capital virtue of childhood.

e. *less strictly.* Main, leading, weighty, important, first-class.

1704 A. COLLINS *Gr. Chr. Relig.* 20 Several capital places in the sacred Writers. 1767 GOOCH *Treat. Wounds* 182 These preparatory rules, generally necessary before any capital operation. 1788 PRIESTLEY *Lect. Hist.* I. i. 5 All history has a capital advantage over every work of fiction. 1793 W. ROBERTS *Looker-on* No. 47 He.. espoused the daughter of a capital grocer. 1818 HAZLITT *Eng. Poets* vi. (1870) 146 So capital and undeniable a proof of the author's talents.

7. In mod. use: Excellent, 'first-rate'. Often as an exclamation of approval.

1760 LD. RADNOR in *Priv. Lett. 1st Ld. Malmesbury* I. 85 The Hobbema is also a very capital picture. 1791 'G. GAMBADO' *Ann. Horsem.* vi. (1809) 91 He clears every thing with his fore legs in a capital style. 1835 T. HOOK *G. Gurney* I. ii, Nobody said capital, or even good, or even tolerable. 1870 E. PEACOCK *Ralf Skirl.* III. 26 He was a capital companion. 1875 JOWETT *Plato* (ed. 2) I. 100 Capital, Socrates; by the gods, that is truly good.

8. Of or pertaining to the original funds of a trader, company, or corporation; principal; *hence*, serving as a basis for financial and other operations.

1709 *Lond. Gaz.* No. 4534/1 An Act for Enlarging the Capital Stock of the Bank of England. 1776 ADAM SMITH *W. N.* I. I. ix. 98 The capital stock of Great Britain was not diminished even by the enormous expense of the late war. 1825 SOUTHEY in *Q. Rev.* XXXII. 41 Compelled.. to encroach largely upon its capital fund. 1884 LD. SELBORNE in *Law Rep.* 25 Chanc. Div. 689 She may commute into a capital sum.. the benefit given to her.. by way of annuity.

III. †**9.** *Capital lye*: the first or strongest alkaline solution employed in the process of soap-making. *Obs.* [Cf. F. *capitel* in same sense, med. L. *capitellum* 'aqua saponis *vel* lixivium', It. *capitello* 'lie to wash and skoure with' (Florio). So that strictly this is a distinct word.]

1704 WORLIDGE *Dict. Rust. et Urb.* s.v. *Soap*, The Magistral or Capital Lye.. is so strong, that an Egg will swim therein. 1731 BAILEY, *Capital Lees*, are the strong Lees, made by Soap-boilers from Pot-ashes.

B. *sb.* [Several elliptical uses of the adjective.]

1. A capital letter. Hence *To speak in capitals*: i. e. with emphasis. (Cf. A. 5.)

1649 G. DANIEL *Trinarch., Rich. II*, cxvii, Noe Character so small, But through that Glass appeares a Capitall. 1676 MOXON *Print. Lett.* 5 A, B, C, etc. are Capitals. 1733 SWIFT *On Poetry* 99 When in Capitals exprest, The dullest reader smokes the jest. 1871 L. W. LOCKHART *Fair to See* I. 4 (Hoppe) 'AND I AM!' cried Fuskisson, a little white ensign, speaking in large capitals, with a voice like a Jew's harp. 1873 BURTON *Hist. Scot.* VI. lxviii. 147 The Service-book was amply decorated with pictorial capitals.

2. A capital town or city; the head town of a country, province or state.

1667 MILTON *P. L.* I. 756 Pandæmonium, the high Capital Of Satan and his Peers. 1750 JOHNSON *Rambl.* No. 49 ¶ 4 He that, like Cæsar, would rather be the first man of a village, than the second in the capital of the world. 1853 ROBERTSON *Serm.* Ser. III. ix. 115 § 2 A constant round from the capital to the watering place, and from the watering place to the capital.

3. A capital stock or fund. **a.** *Commerce.* The stock of a company, corporation, or individual with which they enter into business and on which profits or dividends are calculated; in a joint-stock company, it consists of the total sum of the contributions of the shareholders. **b.** *Pol. Econ.* The accumulated wealth of an individual, company, or community, used as a fund for carrying on fresh production; wealth in any form used to help in producing more wealth.

[1611 COTGR., *Capital*, wealth, worth; a stocke, a man's principall, or chiefe, substance.] 1630–9 WOTTON *Lett. & Treat.* 459 (K. O.) 1647 CLARENDON *Hist. Reb.* VII. (1847) 441/1 Such anticipations upon all kinds of receipts for monies borrowed and already spent, that they had no capital for future security. 1727–51 CHAMBERS *Cycl.* s.v., Power given by Parliament to the South-Sea Company to increase their capital. 1790 BURKE *Fr. Rev.* 51 You began ill.. You set up your trade without a capital. 1793 BENTHAM *Emancip. Col.* Wks. 1843 IV. 411 In proportion to the quantity of capital a country has at its disposal, will.. be the quantity of its trade. 1796 MORSE *Amer. Geog.* I. 442 The gentlemen of fortune turn their capitals into this channel. 1825 McCULLOCH *Pol. Econ.* II. ii. 73 The accumulation.. of the produce of previous labour, or, as it is more commonly termed, of capital or stock. *Ibid.* 114 Credit.. enables those who have capitals.. to lend them to those who are desirous to obtain them. 1863 FENN *Eng. & For. Funds* 26 Bank Stock.. is the capital of the Corporation of the Bank of England. 1874 HELPS *Soc. Press.* iii. 54 The immense difficulty that it is for any human being without capital to ensure himself a living.

c. *Fixed capital*: that which remains in the owner's possession, as working cattle, tools, machinery, etc. *Circulating, floating capital*: that which is constantly changing hands or passing from one form into another, as goods, money, etc.

1776 ADAM SMITH *W. N.* (1869) I. II. i. 276 His capital is continually going from him in one shape, and returning to him in another. Such capitals.. may.. be called circulating capitals. 1825 McCULLOCH *Pol. Econ.* II. ii. 95 What could he do without the assistance of fixed capital or tools?

d. *fig.*; also phrase, *To make capital out of*: to turn to account.

1847 HELPS *Friends in C.* (1851) I. 28 To reject the accumulated mental capital of ages. 1855 MACAULAY *Hist. Eng.* xxv. (1859) IV. 314 He tried to make.. political capital out of the desolation of his house. 1865 MRS. RIDDELL *G. Geith* II. ii. 26 The quietest, most conciliating manners that ever a man made capital out of. 1885 STEVENSON *Dr. Jekyll* i. 8 If you choose to make capital out of this accident.

4. *Fortif.* (See quot.)

1706 PHILLIPS, *Capital*, the line.. drawn either from the angle of the Polygon to the point of the Bastion, or from the point of the Bastion to the middle of the Gorge. 1853 STOCQUELER *Mil. Encycl.*, *Capital*.. is an imaginary line bisecting the salient angle of a work.

†**5.** (See quot.) *Obs.*

1799 G. SMITH *Laborat.* I. 188 One part of capital or cream of clay.

Capital (kæ·pităl), *v.* [f. the sb.] *trans.* To furnish or adorn with a capital.

1851 RUSKIN *Stones Ven.* I. ix. § 29 They shod and capitaled the mouldings till they looked like a group of shafts.

Talonbooks • Vancouver • 1984

published with assistance from the Canada Council

Talonbooks
201 1019 East Cordova Street
Vancouver
British Columbia V6A 1M8
Canada

This book was typeset by Resistance Graphics and printed in Canada by Hignell Printing Ltd.

First printing: November 1984

Earlier versions of some of these stories appeared in *The Capilano Review* and *Prison Journal*.

These stories are fabrications. Any resemblance to actual persons, living or dead, is purely coincidental.

Canadian Cataloguing in Publication Data

Fawcett, Brian, 1944-
Capital tales

ISBN 0-88922-221-5

I. Title.
PS8561.A93C3 1984 C813'.54 C84-091456-3
PR9199.3.F39C3 1984

Contents

The Pigs Treat the Goats Real Fine

In the old days, when people still knew what they were and where they lived, they told a lot of stories about tigers. Tigers, the most popular and ironic of the fables went, treated all the other animals "just fine". They built sturdy hovels for the pigs and goats, and fed them all the nutritious slops they themselves didn't want to eat. Sometimes the tigers went out to the barnyard in their fine striped coats to feed the pigs and goats in person and to discuss important political and philosophical matters with them. Whenever they did this the pigs and goats all quivered inside their itchy skins with fear and delight, wondering at how fine the world was getting to be.

But sometimes, other old-fashioned stories tell us, the tigers would round up all the fattest pigs and the choicest goats, and eat them.

That was the way things were, however ugly it sounds today. The tigers went about preening and purring and occasionally growling loud enough for everyone to hear, and the pigs and the goats kept their noses to the dirt and everybody knew what they were and what they had to do to keep the world safe for their children and for democracy.

•

This is not a tiger story. The tigers have disappeared. Some say they're still around, disguised as other animals, and that they still round up the pigs and goats and eat them, just like they always have. Others say the tigers slipped into the jungle and died, and that the pigs and the goats and the other animals are running things now. I don't know which of these is true and, like I said, my story isn't about the tigers.

Without the presence of tigers, you see, the pigs act with great cunning around the barnyard, and if they're provided with the slightest opportunity, they'll indulge in any manner of obtuse practice in order to relieve the daily tedium of being fattened for slaughter. The free-ranging goats, who by contrast appear more active and sanguine, but actually are neither, also take their greatest pleasures from perverse and monomanial procedures of one sort or another. So when the pigs are left alone with the goats, strange things happen: witness the following.

•

John Yardley wasn't his real name. He changed it when he was twenty-four—"anglicizing" it, as he explained, because he felt that carrying a "mediterranean" surname into a career in project management would identify him with all kinds of lazy and shiftless assholes who would rather lie around behind piles of lumber than put in a good day's work. John was anything but lazy. He was organized in every way, an efficient, ruthless professional if he did say so himself. His colleagues tended to agree with his self-assessment.

J.Y., as he called himself, lived in Akron, Ohio, which, like many places in America of low-angle landscape taken over by the profit-oriented, is a fountain of things dull and sinister. Akron, with its democratic virtue withered to sentimentality and biological warfare installations, is the most accurate landscape for this tale.

J.Y. was single. He was neither divorced, widowed, gay, nor interested in the subject. He'd been with "his share of women", but finally they were not important to him and never had been. They were "okay", and so was sex, but, hey! he could take them or leave them. And it. Sex was, he occasionally pointed out to himself in the shower, messy. And so were women, particularly now that they were making all sorts of absurd demands for equality. These days, he often said to his cronies, there's no way of knowing what you can get away with.

In a small room in the basement of J.Y.'s suburban home lived his widowed mother. J.Y. told his business colleagues that she was his housekeeper, who, even though she was elderly, slow, and barely spoke English, he kept off the welfare rolls because at heart he was a kind and even sentimental man.

At the age of forty, J.Y. was a successful research manager for one of the largest tire manufacturers in the nation. He was physically fit, having installed a weight-room, complete with universal gym and a full wall of mirrors, in an extension to his garage. He'd recently become an aficionado of Japanese culture, and, more recently still, the victim of nightmares. In all these nightmares he was alone and friendless, falling into a darkness that was silent and without end.

The nightmares worried him enough that he consulted the sympathetic wife of a colleague, a woman who dabbled in astrology and tarot cards, but who was nonetheless conventional enough to employ her occult interests as a useful social adjunct to her husband's frequent weekend business barbecues. This woman told J.Y. bluntly that he was worried about dying alone. J.Y. laughed uncomfortably, and the woman became even more blunt: in fact, she said, he was probably *going* to die alone. The reason, she went on, was plain. J.Y. was childless.

When he heard this, J.Y.'s laughter hardened, and he repeated what he had said on the subject at least a thousand times before: no one was going to fence him in. But several days later he asked his mother the same questions and she, rather timidly and in broken English, told him the same thing.

Against his better judgement and his will, the question of children and mortality began to gnaw at him. Marriage, as you can easily deduce, was out of the question. His life did not have room for such a demand on his time and talents. But J.Y. took pride in being a problem-solver, just as his hero Harvey Firestone had been, and he approached this problem as both of them would have approached any problem: with good old American knowhow.

Recently he'd seen a newspaper story about a small and thus far covert industry that might be able to solve his problem. It involved women who, for psychological or religious reasons, could not bear to live without continuously bearing children. They had, in the face of whatever personal circumstances confronted them, begun to satisfy their urge by bearing children for money on behalf of those who could have none of their own and who were unwilling or unable to go through the normal channels to adopt one. If a couple could contract for the production of a particular child, thought J.Y., why couldn't he? It was more or less legal, and it would provide his mother with something to earn her keep by. She would raise it, and he would have an heir and an end to his nightmares.

It wasn't hard to make contact. He searched for ads in a variety of large-circulation newspapers most respectable people wouldn't admit to reading. He followed the ads for several weeks until he decided he could distinguish the real thing from the ads for kinky sex. Then he discussed the legalities with his lawyer, and placed a phone call to a suburb outside Peoria, Illinois.

"John or Rosemary Wertschik?"

"Yes, this is Rosemary speaking."

"I'm calling about your ad."

"Yes. Go ahead."

"I'm interested."

"Okay."

"I'd like some information."

"Sure. Go ahead and ask."

"What's your background?"

There was a hesitation at the other end. "We're decent people. What do you mean?"

"What's your, uh, racial background? Where do you come from? What colour are your eyes..."

The voice cut in, much harder now. "Oh. I'm white. Polish-American descent. I have blond hair, actually, and blue eyes."

"How about your husband?"

"Yeah, well, he's white too," the woman said, coldly. There was a long pause.

"Are you pretty?" J.Y. asked.

There was laughter from the other end. "My husband says I'm

beautiful. Really. I'm okay."

"Well," J.Y. said in his best committee-room voice, "I'm interested in doing business with you. What do we do next?"

"When can you drive out here? We can meet with my doctor. He'll arrange the legal papers and the transfer of semen."

"The what?"

"The transfer of semen. You didn't think I was going to sleep with you, did you?"

"No. Not really." J.Y. had thought about that part of it, and was mildly curious about what it would be like to sleep with a woman under such circumstances.

"Well, I'm a married woman. This isn't some sex thing, you know."

"Yeah, I understand that," J.Y. said, after the slightest of hesitations.

"Well, I hope you do," the voice at the other end said coldly.

•

J.Y. made an appointment for the following week, and said he would phone back before leaving to make sure the doctor was available.

"The doctor will be available. This is business, remember?" the woman reminded him. "You don't need to telephone again. Just be on time."

It was, as a matter of fact, all business. The documents were drawn up, the semen "transferred", the advance cheque written, and J.Y. went back to Akron to wait out the term of the pregnancy. He subdivided his basement again, building a small bedroom for the child off his mother's room. He even improved the kitchen in the rumpus room, replacing the hot-plate with a small stove, and purchasing a new refrigerator to replace the small bar fridge she used.

At full term the child was born, and J.Y. was telephoned to come and pick it up. He took a week off from work, bundled his mother into the car, and drove to the Detroit hospital in which the child had been born.

John Wertschik met him in the hospital lobby. He seemed oddly like the typical father of a newborn infant, nervous and jubilant. But

Wertschik's exuberance vanished when J.Y. asked to see the child before he paid the hospital bills and handed over the final cheque. Only a fool, J.Y. told the man, takes delivery of merchandise before seeing what kind of condition it is in.

The newborn child was deformed. "Hydrocephalic, I'm afraid," the attending intern told him. "There was no way of predicting it. You're the father?"

"Not exactly," J.Y. said, instantly evasive. He was staring at the enlarged dark head and puny limbs of the newborn child, making calculations as fast as he'd ever done in his life.

"How's that?" queried the intern. "How can you 'not exactly' be the father?"

"I'm afraid I'll have nothing to do with this," J.Y. said in as businesslike a manner as he could muster. Then he walked away before the puzzled intern could protest.

•

But it wasn't as simple as J.Y. would have had it. Papers had been signed, and in those papers John Yardley was named as the legal and genetic parent of the unfortunate child. The Wertschiks consulted lawyers, and then the state authorities, and the state authorities stifled their feelings and consulted their own lawyers, and eventually summonses were served. The Wertschiks were not interested in keeping the child, and they were taking the position, with every expectation that the courts would rule in their favour, that legal responsibility for the maintenance of the child fell to John Yardley, the child's father.

"Your only chance of evading the responsibilities of paternity," J.Y.'s third lawyer advised him, "is to deny that paternity. You can prove that you are not the parent if the blood type doesn't match. But if in fact your semen was involved, you're legally responsible."

"No other way to get out?" J.Y. asked bleakly.

"Off the record, you can refuse to take the blood test, and then perjure yourself. But if you did that, with the available documentation in this case, it's unlikely a judge would believe you. You could end up in real trouble."

J.Y. looked at the tasteful furnishings of the lawyer's office. On the wall behind the lawyer was a large painting of a tiger. The animal was lying on its side, and was contentedly licking its striped flank. J.Y. felt as if he'd been victimized, and now he had his back against the wall. What had begun as a mutually profitable business transaction had been turned rotten by forces beyond his control. The tiger painting was oddly comforting, although the tiger seemed completely indifferent to his tribulations.

"We have to fight this injustice," he said, resolutely. "There's no way I can accept a monster for a son."

The lawyer shrugged. "It's your money. You're aware that the child is unlikely to survive beyond the onset of puberty. It might be cheaper just to institutionalize it and wait for it to die."

"I can't do that," J.Y. said, feeling his revulsion turn to righteousness. "It's the idea of the thing I can't handle. I want to be free of this business, completely. I was sold a bill of goods, and the merchandise was defective. I'm going to exercise my fundamental rights."

•

J.Y. had another motive, one that he couldn't discuss with a lawyer. Since the birth of the child a new set of nightmares had begun to assail him, these ones even more disturbing than the others. The damaged child lay sleeping in his living room, its enormous head nearly filling the room, its eyes, malevolent but without intelligence, watching him wherever he went in the house. And, in the nightmares, changes were beginning to occur in J.Y.'s anatomy—his muscles were atrophying, and his head had grown to double its old size. Each time he had the nightmare he awoke in a cold sweat and could not return to sleep, no matter what he did. He spent long and unproductive hours pacing his living room, or examining his body for signs of the changes he had already experienced in the nightmares.

His ordeal didn't affect his performance at work, but it made him more irritable with his mother, who, he began to perceive, had helped trick him into the mess he was in.

The nightmares stopped abruptly when the results of the blood tests came in containing a surprise. The child did not have the right blood type. It was not, therefore, J.Y.'s progeny. He consulted his lawyer, and they decided to sue the Wertschiks for breach of contract, punitive damages and costs. This business, according to J.Y., had already cost him in excess of $15,000, not to mention the value of his time and the considerable mental stress and suffering involved.

In court, the Wertschiks answered the charges by saying that they were unaware that they were required to cease having sexual relations during the period immediately before and after artificial insemination. When several spectators in the courtroom broke out laughing, Rosemary Wertschik smiled demurely.

The judge ruled against them, and the next day they told reporters that the stress of this unfortunate court case had been too much for them: they were bankrupt and would soon be filing documents to that effect. But the next day they simply packed up and disappeared, taking their two children with them. J.Y. also left for Akron the same day.

•

J.Y. is still living in Akron, Ohio, attending barbecues and moving steadily, if somewhat more slowly, up the ladder. He doesn't consult his friend's wife about spiritual matters anymore, and the only things he asks his mother about are when his shirts will be ironed and where his morning coffee is. He will tell you, if you ask, that he is wiser for what happened, and a little poorer. If you're impolite enough to pursue the topic, he will tell you that he prefers not to talk about it.

"Some tragedies are best put to rest and forgotten," he will say.

You can't ask the Wertschiks about any of this because they disappeared.They're probably living in California, because Rosemary often mentioned to her friends that she really always wanted to live in California.

You could ask the child about it, but you wouldn't get an answer. The doctors say he's little more than a vegetable, and that he will never know who or what his parents are. He may never be able to lift his head from the pillow he lies on, to gaze out across the yard where the pigs wallow in the mud and the goats feast on the garbage some say the invisible tigers have left behind.

The Coming of Post-History

First of all, this is a true story, which is to say, it is based on events in the "real" world and I've depicted them as accurately as possible given the fifteen-year interval between their occurrence and this writing. Second, this is a moral tale, which is to say that these events illuminate a space larger than themselves. For me, they signified the first moments in which our civilization could be seen to have stepped outside the continuum of consciousness it has been in since an old Greek named Heraclitus pointed out that it was impossible for a person to step into the same river twice. It is Post-History now, and anything can happen. That you may, as the reader and as your own free agent in the world, have your own notion of when and how Post-History commenced, is not in dispute. I'm offering mine.

•

In the early 1960s, in the far north, a trapper was killed by a large male grizzly bear. The grizzly was swiftly hunted down and killed by the government. During the official hunt for the grizzly, a second man was accidentally killed. That's what the newspapers said about it at the time. The message behind it was the same as that behind almost everything in the newspapers: isn't it awful that such bad things happen and aren't you glad they didn't happen to you. Stay at home, safe in your bungalows, folks.

The trapline the trapper was working ran through the range of an old grizzly, and the grizzly, by accident, had stepped into the heavy steel jaws of one of the traps. He wasn't captive for long, but in escaping from those steel teeth the grizzly lost a good portion of one paw. The wound soon became infected and the animal was unable to forage. Winter was approaching, and the grizzly, emaciated and crippled, was in no condition to survive it.

Now, the native peoples of North America almost universally regard bears, particularly grizzlies, as near-human, treating them with exaggerated respect and referring to them as "our brothers across the river". What all that means, when the mysticism is cut from it, is that a smart human being should stay as far away from them as is practical. For sure, nobody knows what goes on in the mind of a grizzly. They are as unpredictable as they are cunning and powerful, and at the best of times woodsmen give them a wide berth. The trapper, of whose thoughts we know almost as little as we do of the bear's, was aware that there was an injured grizzly on his trapline, and had borrowed a heavy rifle from a friend as a precaution against meeting up with it.

Despite that, as this experienced trapper sat on a log in his camp on the morning after the winter's first snowfall, eating breakfast, coffee mug in hand, the old grizzly moved in behind him and with one swipe of his remaining forepaw, separated the greater part of the man's skull from his neck. The old bear did not maul the body, nor did he eat any part of it as grizzlies sometimes do, and something which, under the circumstances, might have been expected. This grizzly simply walked away. A few hours later, a cousin found the body of the trapper face down in the new-fallen snow, coffee mug still clutched in his hand.

Up to this point, the continuum of History is still secure: it is Modern Times, despite the rustic setting and the pointless death of the trapper. The newly fallen snow is pure and white, the wounded grizzly is hobbling through a glen of leafless poplars several miles from the camp, and we all know what's going to happen next.

We have to kill the bear, right? And while you, the reader, are thinking about why we have to kill the bear, sure enough, in the dead trapper's camp, several people are trying to decide how best to accomplish just that. To track the animal on foot, they know, will be extremely dangerous. The bear has already demonstrated how wily it is and there are, in fact, few animals on the planet more cunning and savage in such a situation than a grizzly.

It happens that on this particular day, in the nearest town, is a government hunter whose job is to kill wild or domestic animals who have become either a nuisance or a danger to public safety. The task will fall to him.

He is radioed, and the next morning he arrives at the trapper's camp in a helicopter. He steps out of the chopper carrying two weapons, one a conventional high-powered rifle with a scope, the other a ten gauge shotgun which he has loaded with solid slugs almost the size of a roll of nickels. To avoid danger he is going to track the offending grizzly with the helicopter—a task made simple by the carpet of new snow. It will, he estimates, take no more than several hours at most, and he invites the trapper's cousin to join him. Revenge, he smiles, will be quick and sweet.

The helicopter lifts off, and, flying just above the treetops, begins to follow the trail left in the snow by the grizzly. The tracks are easy to see with binoculars, and within half an hour the animal is spotted. The helicopter pilot, with some difficulty, flushes it out into a moose-meadow where the hunter can get a clear shot.

Now the helicopter hovers, about thirty feet in the air and perhaps fifty feet from the grizzly, who stands on his hind legs, angry and at bay. The hunter lifts the shotgun, aims quickly and fires, knocking the grizzly down. He pumps the empty shell out, aims and fires again in the same motion, repeating this procedure four times until the animal is clearly dead, little more than a hulk of ripped flesh. The score is even, Justice has been served, and the pilot sets the helicopter down so they can give the carcass a quick examination. After that, they will load it onto the rails for a more thorough examination in the laboratory. Revenge is not enough: they must know why the bear killed the trapper, to see if there is some scientific pattern that can be detected.

The government hunter is eager to begin this part of his work. He is so eager that he leaps from the helicopter before it is firmly on the ground. The machine dips back as his weight leaves it, and then dips forward again in compensation. On the second dip, the rotor clips the top portion of the government hunter's skull and removes it. He is dead before his body hits the ground.

•

I can't be precise about the exact moment when Post-History began. It was somewhere between the time I first encountered the facts of this tale, and the moment when this story began to take shape. Like almost anyone, I feel sorry for the trapper's family and friends. Such sympathies, however, leave me within History. Then other questions creep into my considerations. Why was the trapper there, and why did he set those traps? For the grizzly I feel less, but I do register the fact that there are far fewer bears than human beings, and quite probably fewer bears than there are men hunting them with guns. As for the government hunter, well, he was the occasion of an unfortunate accident, a pointless loss of life. But if he had not pursued the bear with such technological enthusiasm, he might still be alive today.

History didn't end nor Post-History begin with any of the above: not with the violence of the events, not with the sympathy for the victims, not even with the ambiguous moral sequencing of it all. And we already know, deep in ourselves, that those dark kindred are waiting for us across the river, just as we all know that there will be no absolute migration in either direction. In this story, there is no place to stand, no place to sit, and there are no exits. There is only Post-History. And that is the story.

Living Together

"Hey, come look!" Garth yells. "There's another party going on outside the Columbia!"

The Columbia Hotel is one of the tougher bars in town, a crossroads for loggers and Indians, hookers and drunks—a fine place for anyone looking for trouble and a vortex for those who know little else. For us it's a good place to watch; good laughs, good fights, lots of traffic in and out, down and away.

We're right across the street in Peterson's Men's Wear, two white boys minding the store. Me and Garth. Art, the boss, is out having coffee.

The waiters have thrown a drunken Indian out of the bar, and he isn't about to walk away from it. By the time I finish what I'm doing and come to the window he's headed back into the bar for the third time. The waiters are starting to get rough.

The drunk charges the entrance, trips on the cement step and slams against the heavy double doors. Like most drunks he doesn't put out his hands to stop the fall, and his face hits the door with a clunk we can hear across the street. He gets to his feet and turns around. He's dazed and there is blood coming from his nose, splattering down the front of his filthy white shirt. He staggers along the sidewalk to the lobby, and is pushed out of there, not roughly, by the desk clerk. There's nothing the drunk wants there anyway so he doesn't protest much.

"He's just catching his wind for another run at the bar," Garth says, as if he were a television commentator at a sports event. "The fun isn't over yet."

The waiters must have thought he'd given up, though, because when he crashes through the double doors for the fourth time he disappears for at least ninety seconds. Then both doors bang open, and they're carrying him, almost solicitously, each with one hand on his shoulder and the other on the seat of his pants. They swing him back and let him go from the step. The skinny body arcs out over the sidewalk and lands with a thump on the hood of a taxicab, spins across it and flops onto the pavement in a heap in front of an oncoming pickup truck.

The pickup stops. The driver, a big meaty-looking guy wearing an oil-spotted baseball cap, hops out, picks up the drunk and throws him back across the hood of the taxi and onto the sidewalk. He grins and yells something to the growing crowd of spectators, then leaps back into his truck and drives off.

The drunk, meanwhile, is on his feet and is weaving around the sidewalk in wonky circles. The cabbie has come out of the bar and the drunk waves at him vaguely, as if to say none of it is his fault. But the cabbie doesn't buy it, and slams him hard against the hotel's brick facade. The drunk collapses, and stays down until the taxi leaves.

I look across at Garth. He glances back and shrugs, as if to say it's the way the universe works, and that there's nothing he can or should do about it. Or maybe he isn't thinking anything like that. Maybe he's just watching, and it's either amusing or it isn't. Maybe I'm doing the same thing.

"What the hell is this, anyway?" I say, a little louder than I need to.

As if in answer, the drunk stands up once more and lifts one foot onto the step of the bar with exaggerated care, brings the other foot up and loses his balance, weaving along the step almost elegantly before he falls backward onto the sidewalk. Finally, he crawls to his knees, pulls himself up on one of the doorknobs and pushes open the other door. He tries to fall inside but one of the waiters has been waiting for him; an arm lashes out, the fist catches him squarely in the mouth and he goes over backward, stiff-legged, out cold.

"Jesus Christ," Garth mumbles.

"What the hell," I reply. "It's none of our business if the crazy bastard wants to get himself killed."

Just then, Art comes in the rear entrance, back from having coffee, and Garth calls him over. The three of us watch the drunk make it up to one knee and try to stand again. His head is slathered with blood, front and back, and he's bleeding profusely from what looks like a broken nose. He staggers up, falls, and then, giving up all pretense of dignity, crawls toward the doors of the bar on hands and knees.

When he reaches it the doors open and two waiters drag him inside. The doors slam shut behind him.

"Well, that's that," Art says. "Back to work."

Garth looks at me. "Just another drunk Indian," he says.

"I guess," I reply, wondering whether it happened because he's a drunk or because he's an Indian.

We know what's going to happen next. The waiters will take the drunk out behind the hotel, beat him unconscious and leave him in the alley. Sooner or later the cops will come along and throw him into the meat-wagon and he'll spend the night in the jug—or in the hospital if he's hurt badly. There are no customers in the store so Garth and I go for coffee.

It's Friday, and the store is open until nine p.m. While we're locking the place up at closing time, I see two Indians walking up the street toward us. The smaller of the two men suddenly punches his companion, who crumples against the store facade. Then he kicks him, in the head, twice, three, four times and walks away. But just as abruptly, he returns and helps his barely-conscious friend to his feet, who paws ineffectually at the bruises that are exploding across his face and mumbles something we can't hear. We watch them stagger arm-in-arm, across the street to the Columbia.

Art tells me to hose the blood off the sidewalk so there won't be a mess in the morning, and I do what he asks, watching it flood, diluted, over the curb and into the gutter. I put the hose back and lock the store, and Garth and I follow the trail through the dark streets of town, beneath the smouldering stars.

The Friend

Bobby barged into my place without knocking and shook me awake.
"Jesus Christ," he demanded belligerently, "why are you lying in bed?"

"Why not?" I mumbled, seeing that he was drunk. I had no excuse for being asleep. It was about as much fun going to bed at nine p.m. on a Saturday night as it would be driving around in Bobby's car drinking warm beer and looking for trouble.

"There's a party," he said with the same challenge in his voice. "Let's go."

"You got any booze?" I asked.

"Yeah," he said, "I've got a case of beer. Come on. Let's go."

"Where's the party?"

"Near here. We can walk, it's only a block. Come on."

I got up and began to dress, pulling on my pants and boots first.

"Okay, I said. "It's your show."

I put on a shirt, tugged my heavy coat over it and followed him outside. We walked across the alley to the grimy cafe next door, shoulders hunched against the April drizzle, the last of the snow rotting in the corners of everything, the winter-killed cars glistening under the mercury lights of the parking lot, the bare trees dark and tarnished with smoke from the mills. We slouched into the cafe, banging into the waiter as we walked down the aisle. Bobby pushed me into a corner booth near the front window. I looked out into the street groggily while he ordered coffee.

I was feeling reluctant about having to go to this party. There would be too many people I didn't know, too many people I knew and didn't much like. Even the thought of girls didn't attract me, but then I remembered, maybe, maybe the one I liked, the waitress with the soft face and small, strong body would be there. Maybe, because someone said she hung out with those guys. But then, no, I'd heard she was sick, rumours of an abortion. And what chance would I have anyhow?

"What the hell are you dreaming about?" Bobby asked, still belligerent.

"Nothing." I replied. "Who's going to be at this party?"

"Nobody. A bunch of assholes, what else?"

"Any girls you know about?" I asked, hopelessly.

"The same ones who hang around with those guys all the time," he told me without much interest in his voice.

"Why are we going, then?" I mumbled.

He didn't have an answer, but I knew that wasn't going to change anything.

•

The coffee came and we drank it silently. I counted the passing cars. I did that a lot in here. As usual, I recognized many of the cars. The same guys were always out on Saturday night.

It had rained that afternoon and now, underneath the artificial lights, it looked as if everything was covered with a kind of slime. Spring was coming, but it was still a month away, and the slime wasn't totally in my imagination. Everything was filthy this time of year, even the window I was looking through was flecked with six months of winter grime. The cars pushed the slick darkness before them, and then the darkness closed in behind them. More cars passed, and more coffee came, and we drank it without talking. It tasted of white sugar and metal.

"You ready?" Bobby asked, as we finished our second cup.
"I guess so. Let's hoof it."

•

We walked back through the alley to get the beer out of Bobby's car. I considered telling him I didn't want to go to his stupid party, but something in the way he was acting stopped me. He opened the trunk of the car, yanked the beer out and slammed the lid shut. I followed him down the alley, feeling like Tonto. He crossed to the other side of the street and walked into another alley, this one clogged with cars. I caught up to him, and we picked our way across a back yard jammed with more cars. He opened the door of a large dilapidated house, and we stepped into its smoke-filled kitchen.

The room was packed. More than a dozen guys were standing around, all of them drinking hard and waiting for something to happen. I picked out one of them right away, a guy who made a special point of disliking me. I didn't like him much either, but since he was tougher than I was my feelings didn't count for a lot. He caught my eye and I looked in another direction. I weasel-eyed the wall, the ceiling, my shoes, anything. What fun, I thought.

Bobby and I edged our way across the room, uncased our warm beer into the refrigerator, and opened a couple of cold ones. I noticed my pal detach himself from the guy he was talking to and head in our direction. He closed in, stopped, and made a big production of officially noticing me.

"Who the fuck invited you?" he growled.

"God did," I smirked. "Fuck you, Ugly."

I turned aside and ducked at the same time, and Bobby stepped across us and punched him before he could hit me. It was a good thing. Just because I'd lipped off didn't mean I was prepared to fight. I'd shot my mouth off because there really wasn't anything else I could do, and he knew that when he challenged me. I figured the fight would get broken up before he got a clean punch in, and that's why I ducked. But Bobby had popped him hard, and he scrambled up from the floor swinging wildly. His friends grabbed him, and Bobby grabbed me and threw me toward the door.

"Let's get out of here, jerkhead," he snapped.

I didn't argue. It had been a great party.

•

Once again I'd have preferred to go home, but we had a case of beer chilling in their fridge and I knew Bobby wasn't going to leave it behind.

"Let's hike it," he said. It wasn't a suggestion.

"Where to?"

"Around the block a couple of times. They'll cool down."

"I hope they all die of alcohol poisoning."

"Yeah sure. But not on my beer."

We circled the block a couple of times silently. Something was eating at Bobby, but he didn't want to talk about it and I didn't ask. There wasn't much point in discussing the street. The trees had been empty since last fall, and the most interesting thing about the remaining snow was the number of piss-holes.

The party had forgotten about us by the time we re-entered. I couldn't see Ugly, and I thought maybe he'd left. I opened the fridge, pulled two beer out and opened them. Bobby stood guard. When I handed his beer to him I noticed that his eyes were bright, almost as if he were near tears. He sneered at my shaking hands when I handed him his beer, then turned his back on me and ambled into the next room.

I followed him, and we made the obligatory circuit through the house. Ugly wasn't around, but then neither were any girls who weren't clinging to their boyfriends. It was mostly guys, and most of them were drunk. There were some empty chairs in the living room, but I didn't sit down. I already felt like a target, and I didn't want to be an easy one.

We made the rounds of the house without incident, and returned to the kitchen. Bobby started a conversation with an Australian guy we'd both seen around town lately. The Australian was fresh out of the bush and full of his beard and logging-camp toughshit disagreeableness. I was about to tell him to fuck off, go brag his toughshit somewhere else, when he snarled at Bobby over something. Without the slightest hesitation Bobby backhanded him, and he went pitching backward down the stairs he'd been foolish enough to stand in front of. I saw his head slam against the concrete floor at the bottom with a visceral crunch. I heard a shriek, and looked up just in time to catch a glimpse of someone throwing something in our direction. I ducked without thinking, and it shattered in Bobby's face. He stared in the direction it'd come from for a second, then turned to me. There was blood spurting from a deep cut almost exactly in the centre of his forehead.

"Some asshole threw a beer bottle at you," I yelled, as if I were telling him something he didn't know. I hadn't seen who'd thrown it, and I didn't look now. I had more immediate things to worry about. Someone handed me a dishtowel to stop Bobby's bleeding, and while I was trying to wrap it around his head I saw the Australian at the bottom of the stairs go into convulsions. Panic set in, guys were scrambling out the door, but someone who had the presence of mind to realize the Australian had swallowed his tongue pulled him onto his back and got his tongue back into position. We got him and Bobby into a car, drove out of the jammed alley and on to the hospital.

•

The hospital wasn't far away, but when we got to it there was a rigmarole to face: What is this man's name, does he have medical insurance, what happened? I didn't know who the Australian was, and I said so. He wasn't carrying a wallet and he wasn't doing any talking either. The two guys who drove us to the hospital decided to take off before someone took the licence number of the car, and so I had to do the arguing.

"I'm afraid this man can't be admitted," the night nurse said.

"Look, lady, you have to take him. He's probably got a fractured skull."

"Well, you'll have to tell me what happened."

"A fight, sort of."

"These two?"

"No, not exactly."

"Oh," she said, deciding that everything I was telling her was a lie, and that I was the villain. "Yes. I see."

Bobby was lying on a gurney holding a large piece of blood-soaked gauze against his forehead, cursing softly and picking at the drying blood that covered his face while fresh blood dropped across his temples and into his hair. I filled out the forms for him and a doctor patched him up, putting in four or five stitches and then taking off without saying a word.

A nurse came in and tied a large bandana around his head.

"The doctor wants an X-ray of your skull," she said.

Bobby looked over to where the Australian was lying. He was still unconscious.

"X-ray his skull," he said, pointing at the Australian. "I don't need any of that radioactive shit. I'm okay."

The nurse shook her head, and retreated from the cubicle. Bobby motioned for me to come over.

"Let's get out of here," he said as I leaned toward him.

I sensed that there wasn't any point in arguing with him now, just as there hadn't been earlier. I helped him put on his coat and we walked out, over the protests of the nurse.

"You can't just leave this man here!!"

"Why not?" I said as I pushed the door open for Bobby. "I don't know him."

•

We'd been deserted, and I wasn't going to go back inside to phone a cab, so we had to walk the mile or two back to my place. I didn't mind. I wanted to put some fresh air between myself and that party, and I figured a walk might help Bobby cool down a little. It was a silent walk. Neither of us felt much like talking.

"Did you see who threw the bottle?" I asked, as we reached the alley behind my house.

"Nah."

"Let's go over to the cafe," I suggested, "A coffee would be good right about now."

"No," Bobby mumbled, "I want to get my car."

"Don't. You shouldn't drive."

"No, I want to, goddamn it."

"Well, let's have a coffee first, okay? I want to make sure you're okay."

"You do what you want, asshole. I need to be alone for a while. Just let me sit for a few minutes and I'll come over."

He climbed into his car and started the motor without waiting for me to reply. I thought he'd take off, but he didn't. I leaned against the driver's window, wondering what to say next. He didn't roll it down, so I walked over to the restaurant alone.

•

It was deserted. I sat down in one of the booths, ordered coffee, and watched the road. The rain had stopped and it was starting to freeze. The greenish light from the mercury lamps forced a weird clarity onto the street. The air was suddenly clear and light, and the traffic was no longer groping its way along, but plunging down the hill toward the river.

Bobby came in half an hour later, pale and looking a little bit like a wounded war hero with the white bandana tied around his head. A red patch had appeared over the cut. I wondered what was going on inside his head, what he'd been doing in the car, but I didn't ask.

The place was filling up now: the drive-in movies were getting out, and the place was full of people with dirty winter jackets and sleepy, half-drunk faces. Outside, a customized blue Ford pulled up and we watched someone get out of it, a tall guy. I thought I recognized him from the party, but before I could be sure, Bobby was out of the booth and running.

They met just outside the door. Bobby didn't stop, didn't say a thing, just swung a left to set him up. The guy's arms came up automatically to block it and Bobby threw a right at eye-level, went through his guard, and caught him. As soon as I realized what was happening, I got out of the booth, threw a dollar bill on the counter and went outside. I had no plan of action. I wasn't going out to watch the fight or to stop it—no one was going to stop this.

Bobby was circling, holding the air tight in his lungs, and then he went in, fast, an exchange, the dull thud of flesh trapped between colliding bone, a graceless sort of sound, and then four or five punches that his opponent didn't block and didn't return, and he went down on his ass, hard, tried to get up but before he could get to his feet Bobby kicked him under the chin, snapped his head back, and that was it, I thought. He went back, smack, against the black pavement, out.

Bobby moved after him, and I saw he was going to put the boots to him.

"Hey, cool it," I yelled. "He's out, can't you see? He's had it."

Some others helped me grab Bobby and hold him. I held his shoulders and he glared at me.

"It's okay," he said softly. "It's cool, I got him."

We let him go and he turned his back to the crowd. We stood staring at each other, our breath shooting out in clouds into the cold air.

"What shit," Bobby mumbled, half turning away from me and putting his knuckle to his nose to test for blood.

Over his shoulder I saw a flurry of movement and a kind of surprise on the spectators' faces, and then there was a howl of rage, and the guy was on him, over him, up on his shoulders and tearing at the bandana. Bobby twisted and swung an uppercut, but the hands got to his face, ripping at his eyes and at the stitches. Bobby threw him off and went at him. There was a blur of punches and Bobby pushed him up against the side of the building and held him by the throat, smashing at his face until the hands dropped, and he hit him on the side of the head and knocked him sideways, down, and Bobby fell on top of him, knees churning, got up and kicked the huddled figure again and again, until there was a perfect ring of people watching and he slowed down, took more care, stood back and stepped in soccer-style, kicked the guy in the side, and then in the face, then in the side, then in the face until sirens wailed in the distance and the the crowd began to disperse, reluctantly, one by one, until there was only Bobby and me and whatever it was on the ground, and the scuff-thump, scuff-thump of the kicking, and I saw the thing on the ground begin to lose its features, blood and bits of broken teeth began to trickle across the pavement as my friend kicked it slowly in the direction of the alley.

•

The cops came in two cars. They put Bobby in the back of one car, and they threw the other guy like a bundle of rags into the back seat of the other car. Bobby sat quietly, blood covering his face and the front of his jacket. I bent over at the window to say something to him, but he didn't look at me. There wasn't anything to say. Now that I needed them, all the words were gone. Bobby stared straight ahead at the red light revolving on the top of the other police car, and the light streaked the windows of the cafe, the silent streets, and whatever was left there in the frozen air.

Willy's Had Enough

Everybody liked Willy. He was big and funny-looking in an overweight, swarthy sort of way and he spent too much time telling jokes that weren't funny. He was also the kind of guy you didn't say anything to unless you wanted everyone in town to know about it. Willy was Italian, or something like that, and he was Catholic, but that was okay as far as we were concerned. We liked him; he let us all have charge accounts in his men's wear store when nobody else in town would even think about it, and he took us for coffee at the cafe next to the store and he gave some of us jobs working in the store on the weekends and after school.

Willy knew a few things, too. He knew all the hookers by their first names because they all came into the store to buy underwear for their boyfriends, and Willy joked around with them a lot, asking them if they'd take it out in trade, and they always laughed like hell and told him sure, he said.

He never took them up on it. They all had the clap or something, he said, although he said he thought about it once when a little blonde named Denise who we all knew actually asked him to have a beer with her one afternoon. Willy said he could see she really wanted it bad, but he turned her down.

"What I can't figure out," Willy said when we asked for more details, "is why they always buy underwear. Can't pimps buy their own?"

Willy was married, and he had a big new house in a subdivision up on the hill, and two kids about four or five years old, a girl and a boy. His wife was Italian too, or at least she was large and dark and had a big nose like Willy's. She was always kind of cold toward us whenever she came into the store to talk to him. Maybe it was just that she was pretty in a way that made us uncomfortable, and that Willy had talked about how much he loved her, and had hinted that there were some pretty interesting reasons why but we were too young and dumb to understand them. He always talked to her in his office, and he was unusually polite around her. He warned us not to joke around while she was there, because, he said, she didn't like him joking around with a bunch of kids.

Willy knew a phone number you could call when you were down at the coast, and this really good-looking woman would come over to your hotel and do anything you wanted her to. What was weird about it, he said, was that she didn't do it for money, so she wasn't a hooker. She just wanted it real bad all the time, he said, and that was the only way she could get enough.

"Anything?" we asked, not really knowing what "anything" meant, but sure from the smile on Willy's face that it must be pretty exotic.

"Anything," Willy confirmed. "You wouldn't believe some of the things she does."

Some of the things he told us she did were pretty strange indeed, and all of us believed him, particularly when he told us the phone number and the name of the woman, even though he admitted that he hadn't actually done any of it himself. He'd been in the next room, he said, but he could hear the noises while his friends did them with her.

We never visited Willy at his house. One of the reasons was that he wasn't around there much, because, he said, he spent most of his spare time out with the kids, or with his two best friends, one of whom owned a logging outfit and the other a lumber mill. Willy went out to the mill every week or so, and spent the day out there, and when either of his two friends came into the store there was a big performance and we got to hear all the latest stories before they went off to finish the day in a bar.

One afternoon, the two friends came in with a guy named Ratson. We all stood around and watched, like we always did, only this time we paid special attention. Ratson was the biggest wise guy in town, and he was always good for something interesting. He flew helicopters for a living and was the youngest, biggest and smartest of a family of famous loggers and hockey players. Handsome smart-asses, Willy called the Ratsons, and the only thing they were better at than slinging bullshit, he said, was getting into fights.

Sure enough, Ratson immediately launched into a story about a woman he was putting the blocks to down in Wilsons Lake—about how he landed his helicopter right in her front yard and then walked in for lunch and a piece of ass for dessert.

"Jeez," Willy said, "where was her old man all this time?"

Ratson shrugged. "The big yahoo works in the bush and never comes out."

Willy looked sceptical. "I dunno," he said. "What if he comes after you? You land a helicopter in somebody's yard and the neighbours are going to know about it."

"Open season on her," Ratson said, by way of explanation.

"Open season on every woman in the area as far as you're concerned," Willy said primly.

We waited for the next shot. None of us had ever seen Willy try to trade wits with someone like Ratson. We were pretty sure Willy was going to lose, and we were curious to see how it would go.

"Aw, look," Ratson said, peering across at Willy and beginning to grin. Willy squirmed. "You go down on your wife, Willy?"

"Christ, no!" Willy squealed. "She's my wife, for Christ's sake."

"Well," Ratson said, stroking his chin speculatively, "you show me a man who doesn't go down on his wife and I'll show you a woman just about anyone can get into."

Ratson put a lot of emphasis on the word "anyone", and when he said it he looked right at us. We all started laughing. Willy laughed too, and then, suddenly serious, told us all to bugger off, that there were customers in the store. He slapped Ratson on the back and told him what a great kidder he was as Ratson walked toward the door with Willy's two friends.

"That's no joke," we heard Ratson say, laughing as he left the store.

•

Most of us assumed that Ratson was right, not that any of us had first-hand information about the subject. When it came up in conversation while we were sitting around the store the next day, Willy said nothing, just looked a little grey around the gills. We guessed he didn't like talking about his real sex life, and it occurred to us for the first time that while he talked a great deal about everyone else's, he never gave us any of the details about his own.

For me, and as far as I could tell, for my friends, sex meant necking at parties and listening to older guys yapping about all the things they were doing. It never occurred to me that when Willy kidded us about all the things we said we were doing he thought we were actually doing them.

So I started making up things to tell Willy, and soon my friends were doing it too, and some of the things we told him were pretty far-fetched. But he lapped it all up, and that egged us on—at least until some of the stories started getting around town, more garbled and untrue even than the way we'd told them to Willy. A few of us got slapped by girls, and one of us got slapped a lot harder by some girl's older brother, and so we quit telling Willy about the things we were imagining we were doing.

Around that time one of his two friends got killed in a freak logging accident, dropping a tree on his own head. We were in the store when the phone call came. Willy hung up and came out of the back room and told us what happened. Then he went sort of blank and started insisting that it couldn't have happened, that things like that just didn't happen. But even we knew they did, particularly to loggers. They happened all the time. But we didn't argue with Willy.

He disappeared for about two weeks; didn't come to the store or anything. I phoned him at home, finally, using the excuse that I had to check with him to see if it was okay to charge up some clothes. The guys at the store were afraid to phone him, and needed to know a whole lot of things so they could keep the place going.

Willy's wife answered the phone. She said Willy was in his suite in the basement, and that even she hadn't talked to him for several days. I asked when he was coming back to work and she said she didn't know, that maybe she would come down to take care of things. Then there was a long silence.

"I think Willy's had enough," she said.

•

Willy came in the next day, but something in him had changed, we could spot that right away. He didn't seem to want to talk, and he didn't, except to ask me when I was going to pay some money on my account. But as soon as he said that he smiled and said not to worry about it, that it didn't matter much. Then he went into the back room and stayed there most of the day.

He seemed to have lost interest in the store, and in all of us. For about a month he came in every few days for a few hours, but after that he quit coming to the store altogether.

Then one day I read in the newspaper that Willy had died of a heart attack. I was upset about it for a little while, and so were my friends, because Willy was our friend, and a nice guy, and he was only about forty years old. That same day a couple of my friends and I ran into Ratson on the street and he told us some strange things about Willy. He said that Willy had been living in his own basement suite for about four years, and that he'd been dead for three days before his wife found him.

"That's awful," I said. "Where'd you hear about that?"

Ratson shrugged. "Everybody knew," he said, with just a trace of mockery in his voice. "Willy never got anything. He was so afraid he might lose what he had, he never even tried."

He hesitated, as if he had something more to say, but then he shrugged again, as if to say, no, you wouldn't understand, and headed up the street to the bar.

I had no place to go, so I followed him until he told me to get lost.

The Ghost

I knew Roger well enough to call him my friend but I don't think anyone but Roger himself would have said they knew the Ghost. And even Roger wouldn't have said he knew what the Ghost was going to do from one moment to the next.

Roger and the Ghost were cousins—their mothers were sisters—and each was the middle child of three. With that, the resemblance ended. Roger was tall, fair-skinned and frecked. The Ghost was dark and stocky. There flowed, in Roger, a stable sap that ordered his outlook in the deepest possible sense. That same sap, in the Ghost, seemed to have soured and run amok.

These fundamental differences multiplied until you began to wonder if similarity of origins dictates anything but acute difference, or, closer in, why Roger and the Ghost could bear to be in one another's company.

Roger seemed born to be a family man. He was responsible, restrained, and he was vigilant of, and obedient to, domestic formalities. He cherished his parents equally and without reserve, and he worshipped his older sister with the same intensity with which he protected his younger brother. The Ghost called him Dagwood, and the truth of it was that there *was* a resemblance, the difference being that Roger was never incompetent and he was only rarely what you could call a funny person. He took things seriously—so much so that if he hadn't been so unquestionably decent he might have been a pain in the ass. But as it was he was a kind of walking counsel, and his loyalty and steadiness were comforting if you were in trouble.

The only loyalties the Ghost seemed capable of was one toward Roger and another toward getting into trouble. He got himself kicked out of home when his father discovered him and his older brother dueling with baseball bats. The Ghost turned the bat on his father when he attempted to break up the fight, putting him in the hospital. His mother then insisted that the police charge the Ghost with something, and when the officers advised the family to work out its problems more peaceably and left it at that, the Ghost took the baseball bat to his mother's best china, then packed up and moved out to the Indian reservation a few miles east of town. There, he said, he could get along with people. He didn't come into town for months after that, except to buy beer and get into fights.

Whenever the Ghost's name came up, adults would shake their heads and look disappointed or stern. Whenever the Ghost showed up I took it as a signal to clear out. That's how he got his name—he showed up only when something bad was about to happen. Sometimes he created the trouble, but usually he just made whatever was potentially violent and ugly ignite. Then he'd vanish.

This went on for several years. Only Roger stuck by the Ghost, and it was only the reputation he'd earned for being civilized that kept Roger from being tarred with the same brush the Ghost was using on himself and everything he could lay his hands on. As it was, the Ghost did a couple of stretches in jail, first at reform school, and when he turned eighteen, in the jail on the hill above town. The charges were always for mayhem of one sort or another—the Ghost wasn't a criminal, he was just crazy. Most of the mayhem fell just short of being funny, as if there was a line within himself the Ghost was trying to walk that kept moving on him. One side of it was foolish and slapstick, the other violent and not quite sane. The strangest incident I saw occurred one Thanksgiving. When he discovered that my family was going to be out of town, Roger invited me for dinner, and, in his typical way, also told my mother he'd take care of me while they were gone. This solicitude didn't exactly fill me with delight. The prospect of a relatively formal dinner with Roger's family was boring enough, but, as dictated by tradition, the Ghost's family would be there too. I didn't know any of them well, and strangers made me nervous. I would have much preferred a cheeseburger at Floyd's Drive-Inn.

Nobody had been able to find the Ghost for two weeks, so I was, in effect, taking his place in the extended family circle. At the dinner table I was even placed next to the Ghost's older brother Dave, who, for as long as I could remember, had referred to me one of two names: Runt and Four-eyes. He had an ugly habit of pulling off my glasses, smearing the lenses, and redepositing them back on my nose a little too vigorously and upside down.

He did precisely that before Roger's father said grace, and it gave me something to do while the ritual droned on. I cleaned my glasses on the tablecloth and put myself behind the eight-ball with both mothers. But I didn't have to stay there long, because suddenly the front door banged open and the Ghost was standing in the living room with a gallon jug of wine in each hand.

"It's me," he announced. "I'm here for Thanksgiving dinner."

Nobody said a word for a moment. The Ghost's eyes scanned the dinner table. Everything was correct, except for one thing. I was sitting in his chair.

"We weren't expecting you," his mother said. She looked annoyed. "Roger tried to find you but you know how that is."

"I was around," the Ghost said. "You just didn't look hard enough." He pointed at me. "Why is he sitting in my chair?"

"He's not sitting in your chair," scowled his father. "You don't have a chair, remember? You broke it over Dave's head the last time you were here."

"He's sitting in my chair," the Ghost insisted, his voice rising.

Roger stood up. "I invited him," he said. "His parents are out of town. So he's not sitting in your chair. He's just sitting at the dinner table. Okay?"

The Ghost seemed to accept the sweet reason in Roger's tone, and his focus shifted from me to the turkey in the middle of the table.

"Nice turkey," he said, as if he were passing an oblique

judgement on a painting or a new car. I saw everyone around the table relax.

"We'll set a place for you," Roger's mother offered.

The Ghost had an odd expression on his face; a feral smile appeared for an instant before it once again went blank. I saw Roger tense, but before anyone could move the Ghost pushed forward, scooped up the turkey in his arms and was on his way out of the room. His father dived at him and so did Roger, and between them they managed to trip him, sending him sprawling along the carpet with the Thanksgiving turkey disintegrating beneath him. The Ghost scrambled to his feet, retrieved one of the jugs of wine, and threw it at his charging father, who ducked. The jug shattered against the wall, drenching the Ghost's mother, who let out a howl of anguish that blended with the Ghost's father's enraged roar and the laughter of the Ghost as he escaped out the door.

I stayed in my seat, paralyzed. One part of me wanted to laugh, and the other part of me wondered if the Ghost had planned the whole thing. He had, after all, left the door open when he entered. I decided he couldn't have planned any of it—it was too spontaneous and too weird. I'd seen that look on his face before. It appeared whenever the scrambled logic he operated with was about to light his fuse.

The table, the house and Thanksgiving itself was a shambles. Roger took charge. He retrieved the abused turkey—as much of it as he could—and instructed those who needed to to get changed, and somehow, more or less singlehandedly, he got his parents and his aunt and uncle calmed down. His uncle wanted to phone the police, but Roger argued successfully that it wouldn't help; the police had told them before to work it out amongst themselves. They were a family, he reminded them, and they had to grin and bear it.

The next morning the Ghost showed up with six of his cronies from the reservation in a beat-up pickup with twenty-two frozen turkeys in the back. They stacked them on the front step, the Ghost knocked on the door, and they all jumped into the truck and disappeared.

Roger told me about it later. No one could figure out where the Ghost got the turkeys from. It was Sunday morning, and the stores were closed. Roger's mother phoned the police, assuming that the

Ghost had stolen them, but no break-ins had been reported.

The mystery didn't get cleared up for a long time, because a week or two later the Ghost left town. Not even Roger knew where he'd gone, and it was a full year before the Ghost bothered to write. He'd joined the U.S. Marines, and he was in Vietnam. He'd arrived just as the first big escalation of the war began, and he was enjoying every minute of it.

The Ghost was in Vietnam, on and off, for three years. Roger, in the meantime, got married, and settled into a job as the assistant manager of the local supermarket. His second daughter was born just a few weeks before the Ghost returned from his final tour of duty. And as far as Roger was concerned, it was as if the Ghost had never been gone.

But the Ghost had changed. The wildness was still there, but it was as if that wildness had met its match, and was tired. He stuck pretty close to Roger's place, helping out with the babies and the cooking and the cleaning, and generally making himself useful and welcome. He got along immediately with Nola, Roger's wife, who had not met him before and had only heard the stories about him. He made no attempt to see his parents or his brother and sister, and although the latter two had been frequent visitors at Roger's, they stopped coming around after the Ghost arrived.

I went over one evening several weeks after his return. After a few beer, the Ghost began to talk about his experiences in Vietnam. He'd spent twenty-two months in combat, mostly north of Da Nang. I got the impression that he'd been in on a lot of dirty details—probably his way of keeping out of military prison.

"What do you guys know about modern ordinance?" he began the conversation.

I shrugged. "Not much. What is it?"

"Ordinance? Oh. Weapons. Guns. You take that little 30-30 of yours," he said gesturing in Roger's direction. "If you're really good, you might be able to squeeze off six shots in ten seconds. The slugs are made out of lead-steel alloy, and they're travelling somewhere in the neighbourhood of 1000 feet per second. When they hit something there's little surface impact and the slug will travel right through to the other side and out, unless it hits a bone, in which case it'll simply ricochet in a new direction. An M-16 fires thirty slugs in five seconds. The slugs are travelling at about 3000 feet per second, and they're made of softer alloy. They also travel end over end. I've seen one of those little rice-grinders get hit in the shoulder, and because of the muzzle velocity and the wobbling and so on, it took most of his shoulder off. If you get hit you're liable to die of shock before you can bleed to death.'"

"Jesus Christ," Roger said, disgusted. "I thought that sort of crap was outlawed. Aren't those the same thing as dum-dums?"

A dum-dum was a soft lead slug with a hole drilled in the end of it. It tended to shatter on contact with a hard surface. Lazy hunters we knew used them to make sure they killed the animal they were shooting at, even though it sent shards of lead all through the carcass, often making the meat inedible.

"They're five times as destructive as dum-dums," the Ghost answered cheerfully, "but they're totally legal. Everyone uses them. Us, the Cong, the Chinese, the Russians, everybody."

"That's crazy," Roger said.

"The world is crazy," the Ghost corrected. "Crazy like a shithouse rat. Everybody is out to get everybody, and there ain't half enough holes to crawl into. You wouldn't believe it."

He opened another beer, sucked back on it and settled back in his chair.

"Listen to this. We were on a sweep—I guess it was about eight months ago. We did it all the time, but mostly we didn't see a thing. We'd get a report they were somewhere, and by the time we got the damned report they were packing up. By the time we got there, they'd have vanished, like into thin air. But this once, we stumbled right onto one of their field hospitals. They'd already left with the wounded who could move; they knew we were going to find the hospital. But they left about twenty-five of the grinders behind. I guess the Cong took all their morphine with them too, because when we showed up most of the grinders were singing like canaries. The CO sent the medics in to do what they could. The first guy they touched blew himself up and took two medics with him."

"The fucking bastards had wired every one of them with grenades. The crazy thing was that they were all lying there grinning like monkeys, waiting for us to come closer so they could take some of us with them. It didn't seem to matter to them that they'd die too."

"What'd you do?" I asked.

"Me and another guy opened up on them with our M-16s. Blew the whole fucking works of them away. Then we called in an air-strike and got the fuck out of there."

I was getting apprehensive. The Ghost had the same look in his eyes I'd seen the night he grabbed the turkey. But it wasn't *quite* the same. It was as if he knew what the turkey felt like now. Roger must have spotted it too, because right out of the blue he asked the Ghost where he'd gotten those frozen turkeys he'd left on the front porch the morning before he left.

"Oh yeah," said the Ghost, laughing. "I ran into a poker game that night. One of the guys playing was one of those poultry wholesalers. He ran up about 200 bucks on me, so I took some of it in turkeys. He had them sitting outside in a freezer truck. It seemed like a good idea at the time."

•

The Ghost got a job, but he didn't seem interested in moving out of Roger's place. There was a rumour going that he stayed around because he was in love with Nola. If that was true, he didn't let on. I was around there as much as anyone outside the family and I didn't see anything. Triangles are always easy to spot; there's a tension in the air that excludes outsiders. I was always made to feel at home whenever I was there, by all three of them. I think the Ghost stayed with them because it was a good place to be, and maybe because he believed that Roger was keeping him straight.

Roger, in turn, accepted his new responsibilities with his usual gravity. He made it look easy, but I don't think it was as easy as it looked. A wife, two small children, one of them newborn, and a newborn Ghost all in one house, plus a steady stream of dependent friends like me—it would have wrecked a less orderly man even if he were a saint.

So Roger instituted a complex set of organizational regulations around the place. Anyone who came around was expected to help; if you stuck around very long, you acquired responsibilities. I was expected to cook dinner occasionally, and to make sure the house was supplied with beer and kept relatively clear of empties. The Ghost took care of firewood and did all the odd jobs. He was a wizard at repairing things, and he spent his free time working on a variety of strange gizmos that were totally beyond my understanding. The Ghost refused to explain their purposes even though I teased him about the ones that were already stacked in the basement, finished, and as far as I could see, totally useless.

In his own way, Roger understood the gizmos.

"Let him play," he explained to me one night after the three of us had exhausted the beer and the Ghost's storehouse of tales about a world without any rules. "He's trying to sort out the rules."

I couldn't see any connection between the gizmos and rules.

"Everybody has to figure out how the world works sooner or later," Roger said. "And the Ghost is doing it in his own way."

I found that explanation disturbing. It implied that the world operated on a logical basis, and that one could, and maybe had to, figure out what it was. Roger wasn't religious, so he had to be talking about tangible rules that could be discovered by experiment; the human equivalent of laws like the law of gravity, or the laws of physics that allowed telephones and radios to work.

Everything I knew about living with my fellow man was cautionary. I knew how to keep from getting hit by a car, and how to stay out of some kinds of trouble. I was curious about why people did the things they did, and what they were going to do next, but finally I believed it was illogical, irrational and dangerous. To me the present was a malevolent fog. I was inside it, and it had me—I didn't have it. The logic Roger seemed to take for granted eluded me. I tried to explain this to him, but I couldn't even explain my confusion.

"The world doesn't work," the Ghost interrupted from deep inside his haze of exhaustion and alcohol. "Roger works."

"Maybe I'm just more afraid of what happens if the world doesn't work than you are," Roger admitted. "When the world doesn't work I act like it does anyway. People are pretty good if they're given the opportunity," he added bleakly.

This time the Ghost couldn't see the connection.

"People are dangerous when they're allowed to be," he grunted. "There's just no way of knowing who's insane."

•

I'd have preferred to believe Roger's way rather than my own or the Ghost's, but I didn't get much of a chance. Several days after that conversation, the first of a bizarre series of events took place.

Roger was seriously injured in a car accident that killed both his mother and his aunt. He'd offered to drive them out to see some friends who lived thirty or forty miles outside of town. They took his uncle's car, an old Dodge the Ghost had recently spent several days working on as a favour to Roger, and more obliquely, as a favour to his father. As the Dodge was rounding a sharp curve, a tie-rod snapped, and the car went off the road and rolled down a steep embankment into the river. Despite a broken arm, Roger pulled his mother and his aunt from the submerged vehicle. It didn't do any good, because both his mother and his aunt were already dead. They had died before the car hit the water. Roger lost an eye. When the car rolled down the bank his head slammed against the rearview mirror; the mirror shattered, and a shard of glass lodged itself in the cornea of his left eye.

In most cases, a death in the family causes the remaining family members to close ranks against the grief, to become closer to one another. These deaths did the opposite. The family began ripping itself apart, and in their grief each individual began to look for a scapegoat. The Ghost was the obvious one. He'd been working not only on the car, but on the part of the car that had caused the accident—the steering.

Even while he was still in hospital, Roger was forced into the role of arbitrator. The hospital room in which he was meant to rest and recover became, by turns, a courtroom and a battleground. It sounds absurd, but it was true. I tried to visit him, but when I got to the door of his room I heard a fierce argument going on. I waited outside for a while, hoping it would subside, but it didn't. Eventually I left the magazines I'd brought for him with a nurse, along with a note saying that I hoped he was okay, deepest sympathies, and that I would do anything I could to be of help.

Later that same evening he called—there *was* something I could help with.

"They're all blaming it on the Ghost," he said, his voice sounding pressured and tired even across the wires. "No matter what I say, they won't listen. I told them it was my fault if it was anyone's. I drove the car off the road."

The more I listened, the crazier they all seemed. Roger's father was craziest of all. He was neither a very strong nor a very intelligent man, and he'd been dependent on his wife in ways not visible to a casual observer like myself. Now, from what Roger told me, he was acting like an Old Testament prophet, demanding, ironically, an eye for an eye. He wanted the Ghost punished in some unspecified way. It was the lack of specificity that worried Roger.

"Look," he said finally, "try to talk the Ghost into splitting for a while. The Old Man is pretty wacky, and I really don't know what he'll do. He might go after the Ghost if somebody pumps a few beer into him and he starts thinking too hard. Tell the Ghost a couple of weeks will do it. I'll be out of here by then, and maybe things'll have cooled off."

I conveyed the message to the Ghost as convincingly as I could, but he wasn't going to leave.

"Nope," he said, "I stay here. Somebody has to take care of Nola and the kids while Roger's on the grease."

There was a resoluteness in his face that convinced me that arguing with him was pointless. I was still leery enough of him that arguing wasn't something I'd have done anyway, and something else told me I should be frightened of the entire family—there was something almost other-worldly in their behaviour, a kind of undistractable concentration, that I couldn't put my finger on.

"Well, I think maybe you should think about lying low for a while," I counselled, remembering my responsibility to Roger. "At least stay away from the hospital."

The Ghost was silent for a moment, then, without responding directly to my advice, he asked me if I had any old bicycles lying around.

"No." I said, puzzled. "Why?"

The Ghost pushed me through the house and into the back yard. In the corner, covering an area roughly ten feet square was another, and by far the largest, of the Ghost's contraptions. Radiating from a central axle were perhaps a dozen bicycle wheels, all interconnected with extended bike chains, the extensions of which were in turn connected to a variety of mechanical items: a propellor on one, another bicycle wheel on another, a 2x4 on a third, and so on. I stared at it, trying to think of something to say.

"What is it?" I asked, trying not to appear as bewildered as I felt. "What does it do?"

"Nothing much," he shrugged. "The kids can play with it. So far it just kind of goes round and round."

"No," I said seriously. "What is it going to be? I mean when you get it finished."

"Nothing. It'll be interesting to look at." The Ghost frowned, and then looked at me speculatively. "Do you think you can get me some bike wheels?"

"You want more wheels?"

"Well," he said, as if it would explain what I was looking at, "I just want the back wheels."

I said I'd look around for some, and retreated into the house as soon as I thought it safe. Then I got out of there.

•

By the time Roger got out of hospital, the contraption had grown even larger, but the Ghost didn't seem to think it was finished. He tinkered with it constantly, removing a section here, adding it on somewhere else in a different configuration. The second time I saw it I detected a purpose in his tinkering. He meant it to operate in unison, so that turning a single wheel would result in movement all through it, and most of the adjustments he was making were to that end.

Roger ignored the contraption. Maybe the eye still caused him a lot of pain, and maybe he had an inkling of what was to come. In either case, he seemed preoccupied and distant, particularly around the Ghost. He'd been angry when the Ghost didn't clear out like he'd asked him to, but since nothing had happened, I assumed that the riot within the family had subsided.

•

I couldn't have been more wrong. The month or so of apparent calm had in fact fermented a darker brew; and what finally emerged was swift, poisonous, and absolute.

It began when the Ghost went out to the auto wreckers looking for parts for his contraption. Following some obscure impulse only he understood and which afterward would remain unexplained, he decided to strip the old Dodge his mother and aunt were killed in. He removed the steering wheel and two of the wheels, threw them into the back of Roger's car and drove back to town. Within a couple of hours, he'd installed them within the contraption. The steering wheel he placed at the centre of the entire device so that you could sit on a bike-seat, turn the steering wheel, and cause the contraption to function in its bizarre way.

He was putting the finishing touches on it the next afternoon when Roger's father walked into the back yard. Like everyone else, at first he stared at the strange contraption with a mixture of awe and misgiving. About the time the Ghost spotted him, Roger's father spotted the steering wheel.

"Hi there," said the Ghost.

Roger's father brushed past him. "Where did that steering wheel come from? Is it what I think it is?"

"It's a steering wheel."

Roger's father turned and stared at the Ghost.

"I know what it is," he said. "I can't believe anyone would do such a ghoulish thing."

"It's a toy for the kids, that's all," the Ghost replied, trying, in the face of the trouble he could see was coming, to be friendly. "Why don't you try it out?"

•

Roger's father didn't try out the contraption. Nor did he go into the house to talk to Roger. Instead he accused the Ghost of being the Devil, of deliberately killing his aunt and his mother, and subsequently flaunting it by building the contraption. Then he stormed off.

Roger had seen none of this, and the Ghost said nothing about it. He stayed out in the yard, tinkered with the contraption, and waited. Three hours later the two bereaved husbands returned with rifles. They were drunk. The rest of it is unclear. There was a furious argument, four shots were fired, and one of the bullets hit Roger in the face as he stepped in front of the Ghost to protect him. He was killed instantly.

No one ever really agreed on what actually happened. The Ghost told me as much as I know, but all he would say about the shooting was that it was an accident. He wouldn't say, either in court or privately, who fired the bullet that killed Roger. The ballistics evidence was inconclusive: the rifle that fired the bullet belonged to Roger's father, but, strangely, someone had wiped all the fingerprints from it, and all three of them—the Ghost, his uncle and his father—alternately claimed that their memories were confused, and that it was all a terrible accident.

The courts couldn't decide either. The Ghost's father was charged with manslaughter, but the jury acquitted him because the testimony was contradictory on all but one point: it had been an accident. The consensus was that Roger's death was punishment enough for a family already so assailed by tragedy.

Within a year, oddly enough, both fathers were dead. The Ghost's father died of a heart attack, and a few weeks later Roger's father shot himself. He left no note.

The Ghost, for his part, hung on pretty well. He stayed with Nola and the two daughters, and about eighteen months after Roger's death, the Ghost and Nola got married.

As for the contraption, the Ghost finally perfected it. Or at least that's what he said. A few years later, just before I left town for good, I stopped in for a visit. I hadn't seen much of them after the killing; they had a lot of things to work out, and I really didn't have much to offer that would have been helpful.

When I arrived, the whole family was in the back yard. The oldest of the two daughters was nearly six, and when I walked in she was sitting in the middle of the contraption on the bike-seat. Beneath her was a garbled array of gears, all slowly revolving as she turned the steering wheel around and around. And around her the twenty or thirty pinions of the contraption turned, most of them painted in bright colours. I closed my eyes slightly, and in my blurred vision they turned into enormous blossoms in a garden that had been made as utterly coherent and connected as it was pointless and crazy.

The Balance of Nature

I'm going to write this down before I forget. I want to remember it because the doctor says it's important. I'm not exactly sure why it's so important, but every time I think about it I get real angry and I don't know why. I asked the doctor why I get so angry about things, and why I never know when it's going to happen. I was seeing him about the tendons I cut on my wrist, and when I asked him those questions, he looked up at me with a funny look on his face and said, well, maybe the best thing you can do about it for now is to write about whatever makes you angry, right while you're still feeling it, and then look at what you wrote later on when you aren't mad any more. That way you might see it differently.

I've got nothing much else to do, so here goes.

My father is kind of a bastard. I'm not supposed to say things like that—whenever I do the doctors all nod at one another and write in their notebooks. But unless I say what's true right from the start, I won't be able to say much else. It isn't what it sounds like, either. I mean, there's nothing wrong with being a bastard. My father is a tough man—cruel, even. If you make a mistake, he nails you to it, and if you're weak he walks all over you.

I'm sort of like him. It's hard to be, sometimes, and there are times when being that way feels really awful. It used to feel bad almost all the time, but I sort of trained myself to be tougher. I decided that I had to, if I was ever going to be anything in life. My father used to say that you had to decide what you were going to do and then do it without letting anything get in your way.

My brother wasn't like us at all. He didn't care about anything my father and I care about, and he never missed an opportunity to say so. As a matter of fact he was always fighting with my father over something or other, because just about everything my father said, my brother disagreed with, and whatever my father told him to do, he went out and did the exact opposite.

If you really want to know, my brother was nothing but a bloody hippie, full of crazy ideas about how you're supposed to eat and how you're supposed to treat women and so on. He could never keep a job, and he never saved a cent, and wherever he was he made trouble, telling people things he knew they didn't want to hear, or telling people's wives things they shouldn't hear. He kind of screwed up my wife that way. About the last thing she said to me was, why can't you be like your brother.

But I never wanted to be like him one minute of my life. Like I told her to her face, maybe she should have married him instead of me, and done without the house and the car and all those things she was always claiming she had to have. All his intellectual ideas and that filthy language he used around women wouldn't have gone very far at the supermarket.

But I'm getting ahead of myself here. I apologize for it, believe me. With all the pills they give me it's a wonder I can think at all anymore. Let me try to sort out the story from the beginning, and you can decide for yourself who was right and who was wrong. I mean, I know I was wrong about some of it, but I had some reasons for doing what I did, and they were good ones.

•

I've always spent a lot of time outdoors, hunting and fishing and that sort of thing. I worked damned hard, and when you work as hard as I do you have to get away sometimes, get away from the job and the city and the wife and kids. We'd get driving down some back road with the old cut-down 4x4 we had, my pal Merv and I, and we'd have the guns all cranked up and loaded to go and we'd have a gay old time.

Fall's the best time of year as far as I'm concerned. The bugs are all gone, the weather's cool and usually pretty good, and you can get everybody off your back and have some real fun. You might even get something, and then you've got free meat for the winter. Not that I ever needed it, but all the same, if it's there for the taking, you've got to be crazy not to take it. Personally I don't like moose-meat all that much, and bear is just too damned greasy. One spring I ended up throwing out about half a moose. It'd been an old bull and the meat was so tough you couldn't chew it, so I chucked it out. I can still hear my brother saying "If you don't want to eat it, why'd you kill it?"

Well, like I told him, I shot it because it was there to shoot, that's why. Not that I could get something that simple through my brother's thick skull. He hated guns and he never went hunting by himself. He claimed he was deaf in one ear from the time I fired off my old 30-30 right next to his head. He deserved it—trying to keep me from shooting an owl. I scared the piss out of him, actually. I thought I'd die laughing, and he didn't ask to go hunting for years after that.

So you can guess I was sort of surprised last fall when he phoned me up and asked if he could come along the next time Merv and I went hunting. I was kind of suspicious, actually, because it'd been so long since he'd been anywhere near a gun.

Of course he didn't have his own gun. That would have been asking too much. I wasn't about to lend him one of mine either, in case he did something weird, like sticking the barrel into the ground and pulling the trigger. I respect my guns too much to have him splitting the barrel on one, and besides, a good gun costs a lot of money. But Merv had an old 4-10 shotgun that wasn't good for much of anything, and he said my brother could use it. He even gave him some shells, something my brother was too damned cheap to buy for himself.

The minute we got the guns loaded and ready to go, the bugger started bitching at us, giving us a lot of crap about the balance of nature, and how we were upsetting it by hunting.

"Balance of nature, my ass," I tell him. "There is no goddamn balance out here. The only law nature has is survival of the fittest."

"Yeah," Merv chimes in, "if assholes like us run across something out here, it ain't fit to survive, so we're sort of helping out your balance there."

"Only God has the right to kill," says my brother, in this really corny voice like he was a minister in church.

Merv turned around and gave him his best shit-eating grin. "Tell you what," he says. "If you see God running around out there today we'll let you have the first shot at him."

I was beginning to get an idea about why my brother came hunting with us, so I shut him down right on the spot.

"Listen, asshole," I say, "If you don't shut up and stop your goddamn arguing, I'm going to ram that 4-10 down your throat and use you for target practice."

He just sneered at me. "Go ahead. At least that way the animals will have a chance."

Merv had heard us fight before, and he stopped the argument by cranking up the 4x4.

"Hop in, assholes," he hollered, "or I'll go hunting by myself."

•

We had about ten miles of road to track in, and a lot of it was in pretty good shape. It was on one of the good stretches, maybe four miles in, that we spotted the grizzly. Funny thing about it was, now that I think about it, that my brother spotted it first, and when he caught sight of it he damn near jumped out of the truck with excitement.

There really wasn't all that much to get excited about. It wasn't exactly what you'd call a monster—a yearling, maybe, but not much older. Not that anyone ever thinks about those things at the time. As far as you're concerned, it's there, and it's moving, and if you don't kill it it's going to get away on you. The old adrenalin starts pounding through your system, and before you know it you're on automatic pilot. I've heard people say that it's the same thing that makes a good soldier, or a high-wire act. Whatever it is, it's a great feeling. You just react. Everything gets very easy and simple.

Anyhow, when my brother starts to crawl out the window of the truck, Merv pulls over and the three of us are out about as quick as you can spit. Merv and I are trying to spot the grizzly clear, and get our rifles up and ready, but my brother just leaps out and goes ki-yi-ing through the underbrush right after the goddamn thing like it's his best friend and he wants to give it a hug. He's no more than fifty feet from it before the grizzly realizes what's going on, and about that time my brother lands face-first on the ground and starts pumping 4-10 shells at it. At least that's what I think he's doing. But then I notice that the shots aren't going anywhere near the grizzly. He's trying to save the bloody thing from us. The trouble is the grizzly doesn't know that's what he 's doing, and decides to attack.

A grizzly can cross a fifty-foot distance in no time at all, but not as fast as a bullet from a .306 rifle. I squeezed off a shot when it was roughly halfway to my brother. I was using magnum charges that I packed myself, and the bullet hit the grizzly like a truck, knocking it sidewise into the brush. Merv and I couldn't see where the bear landed, but we could sure as hell hear my brother screeching at us, and we could hear the bear thrashing around somewhere close to him. Merv hollered at him to get the fuck out of there. Both of us were wary about another bear, maybe the sow, lurking nearby.

A female grizzly protecting her young, even a yearling she probably wants to get rid of, isn't going to sit around thinking about the right way to do it—she'll just attack, and it'll be all out. I'd do the same thing myself if some sonofabitch was putting the boots to my kid. So I jumped up on the hood of the 4x4 and did a 360 to see if I could see anything. It was one of those things you do without thinking. I knew my brother was okay, and that Merv had an eye on him to make sure the yearling didn't come out of the thicket after him.

One of the things hunting teaches you is not to think too much. If you start thinking too much about what's out there and what can happen, you end up with a moose's horn up your gig. You learn to trust your gun, and when you get good and something happens, you just go into that old automatic pilot. If there was another bear around, I was going to kill it as cleanly as I could. I wasn't about to do the foxtrot or discuss my philosophy of life with it.

As soon as it seemed clear that the yearling was by itself, I got off the truck and walked out to see what had happened to it. I ignored my brother. I was pretty pissed off at him, I'll admit it. Merv could see to the snivelling little jerk if he wanted to. I had a bear to kill.

Meanwhile, everything was quiet over in the thicket the yearling had gone into, and that had me worried. The only kind of grizzly that isn't dangerous is a dead one. I could hear Merv talking to my brother, telling him to get back in the truck and stay out of the way. I walked over to them and offered to break his face with my rifle butt if he didn't. He looked frightened, and for once, he did as he was told.

The yearling must have heard me coming, and as I approached the thicket it began to yowl. It was the weirdest sound I've ever heard in my life. I knew it wasn't human, but all the same it sounded exactly like a kid in pain. That kind of ripped into me. I fired two shots into the thicket, but it just made the yearling scream louder. For a second, just one or two, I felt really sorry for it. Then I heard a grunt from behind us and there was the sow I'd been looking for, standing up on its hind legs right behind the truck. I saw my brother frantically rolling up the windows, but he might as well not have bothered. The sow was after us. She came barrelling around the side of the truck and headed for us on a dead run. I cranked another cartridge into the chamber and took a quick bead on her. The truck was right in behind her, and just as I was about to squeeze the trigger I saw my brother's face, his eyes like saucers, staring at me. It threw off my concentration; I hesitated for an instant and Merv fired two shots. The bear went down just as I fired.

It was like slow motion in the movies. The windshield of the truck shattered in front of my brother's face. A split second later I saw the crazed pattern of the glass begin to change as rhythmic showers of blood sprayed it and slid across the surface and into the cracks. Merv was pumping bullets into the dying sow, and I could hear the yearling's screams as I ran to the truck.

•

Merv kicked the windshield out so we could see enough to drive, and he drove the 4x4 into town a lot faster than it was meant to go. It didn't help. My brother was dead long before we arrived at the hospital. The bullet had hit him square in the throat, severing his jugular. When I got to him he kind of stared at me with this puzzled look in his eyes. Then I watched them go out, slowly, the way a candle sputters out when the wick is finished. He didn't say a thing—he couldn't, I guess, because his vocal cords were gone.

I felt cold, but that was all. Maybe I was in shock, I don't know. Two cops came to the hospital and talked to us. Merv did all the talking and I just sat there, staring at my brother's corpse lying on the gurney until they pulled a sheet over his head and rolled him away. For some reason all I could think of were the bears. I could hear the yearling screaming, right there in the hospital, and it wouldn't stop.

The cops let us go, telling us they'd be in touch in the next day or so, and I followed the two cops and Merv out of the hospital. I felt pretty weird. I was going to have to tell my parents about it—that I'd shot my brother. But that could wait. First I had to see to those bears.

"We've got to go back out there," I said to Merv.

He stared at me as if I was crazy. "Your brother's dead and you want to go back out there?"

"We can't leave that yearling," I said. "It's got to be put out of its misery."

"Fuck the bears," he said. "I'm not getting into that truck again. The whole cab is covered in blood."

"We left the rifle out there," I insisted. "We've got to go. The cops want my rifle."

"Let them go get it. If you go out there after what's happened you're a fucking crazy man."

I could hear that yearling screaming in my ears, and my whole body felt like it was encased in metal.

"You go by yourself," he said. "I'm going home."

I had to go. I know it doesn't make sense, but I had to finish up what we'd started, even if I had to do it alone. Any maybe that was best, anyway. It was my fault in the first place.

I felt under control. I had a flicker of a thought about my father, wondering what he'd do in the same situation. The more I thought about it, the more I thought he'd do just like I was. I could hear his voice saying, 'If you start something, you've got to finish it.' Maybe he was saying other things too, but I didn't hear them. It was like being in a tunnel. There was a place at the end of it I had to get to, and to get there I had to ignore everything else.

By the time I got back to the spot where everything had happened, it was late afternoon. It was quiet as hell. I pulled Merv's rifle out of the back of the truck—he'd left it there when he walked out on me—cranked a shell into the chamber and trotted down the slope with the safety off. The sow was dead. I'd been pretty sure she would be after the rounds Merv put into her. I put another round into her head and went after the yearling. There was a trail of blood and gore leading into the thicket, and judging from that, the yearling was hurt bad. It'd come over, nuzzled around the sow, and returned to the thicket when it got no response. I was hoping that it'd bled to death, but as I got near it started in again with the same weird screams as before. This time, though, I could see it. I had to blast it four times before the screaming stopped.

I waited for a minute or two before I went in. It was dead, all right. I think the earlier shot had broken its jaw; the other four slugs were all in the body, the last through the heart.

I dragged the carcass over to where the sow was and skinned it. After that I took Merv's hatchet and chopped the paws off the sow for the Fish & Game guys, and threw them in the back of the truck with the yearling's pelt and the rifles. Then, sort of on impulse, I went back to get the skinned and gutted carcass of the yearling, dragged it to the truck and threw it in on top of the rest. The damn thing looked almost human, if you didn't look too carefully.

The coyotes and ravens would take care of the sow in a few days. You can only really eat grizzly when it's young, and even then it's usually inferior to black bear. You never know what a grizzly's been eating until you taste the meat.

•

Cleaning up the mess had taken a few hours. I'd had to finish in the dark, using the headlights from the truck so I could see what I was doing. I guess I'd been working so hard I kind of forgot everything, and I was feeling pretty good. Nothing of what I'd done or what I had to do had really hit me—I was too busy doing what I was supposed to do, and that always keeps you from thinking too much.

On the way back to town I started thinking about what was next. The first thing was to drive over to my parents. There was no getting away from that part of it—that or telling my wife. What I'm trying to get at is, there weren't any rules for what I had to do next. I mean, how do you just walk in and tell your father you shot your brother?

It really does sound nuts now that I've written it down, but it wasn't. It was an accident, and it was the accident that was crazy. Maybe it was all that stuff that made me turn around when I was almost at my parents' house and go home. I suddenly realized I had to get the carcass up on a hook so it would drain properly—otherwise the meat wouldn't be worth shit.

I was hanging it in the garage when my wife came out. I saw right away she knew, because she was as white as a sheet and she'd been crying. She stood there watching while I finished hanging it, and the tears were streaming down her face. Then she started after me like a crazy person, screaming that I was a bastard and that I wasn't human, and pounding at me. I guess I came apart; like, maybe I really was crazy for a minute there. Anyway, I had Merv's hatchet in my hand because I had to chop a hole in behind the bear's tendons for the rope, and I just up and swung the hatchet at her without thinking.

•

There's some other stuff, but I don't remember it. I sort of remember phoning the cops, and then my father was there, and I remember that he was staring at me. Maybe what I've forgotten will all come back later.

•

I wish my father would come. I want to talk this over with him. I don't know what I did that he wouldn't have done in similar circumstances.

Arctic Plums

When I was a kid, a woman named Gladys Snow lived in a small white house with a big yard a couple of blocks away from my house. She died a short time ago, and that's what made me think of her. I never thought of her as a friend, and the only time I ever spoke to her was when I used to collect money for the local newspaper, and even then we had little to say to each other; a bad-tempered old lady and a barely curious young boy.

The only questions I might have wanted to ask her would have been about her garden, and why it was so odd. There were things in her garden no one else in town had, and I was curious about them. Most of the neighbourhood kids believed Gladys was a witch, and my older sisters claimed that every plant in her garden was poisonous—that was why so many of them were always withered and dead, even in the middle of the summer.

Neither of these stories was true. I knew that because I got to walk through the garden twice a week to deliver the paper, which meant that I got as close to the plants as any neighbourhood kid ever did, and I was the only one who had time to look. Most of the plants in her garden I knew from helping my mother in our own family garden. I'd even have known what most of the dead ones were and where they came from if I'd bothered to think about it.

Each spring a delivery truck arrived at Gladys' house and unloaded boxes of plants. Most of the boxes came from the States, and a few of them, the smaller ones, came from England. Some of the plants she got were roses. I knew that because my father grew roses too, or tried to. Every year he ordered plants from the catalogue, every spring they arrived and were planted, and every winter they died. I never asked my father why he kept on planting roses every year, and it's too bad I didn't. If I'd asked, he might have given me a clue to what was going on in Gladys Snow's garden.

But, as I said, I didn't ask him. I assumed that my father had a good reason for what he did, even though each spring he would let fly with some truly eloquent curses as he pulled up the previous year's dead roses. He cursed the roses, the company that sold them, and he cursed the bitterness of the climate, and for all I know he might have cursed Luther Burbank himself. But since he cursed at a lot of other things too, I didn't see anything special about his maledictions over the dead roses.

If I'd been paying attention, I'd have noticed that the dead plants in Gladys Snow's garden were the plants that had come in the boxes from England and the States. Nearly all of them died: spindly little vines, misshapen saplings, even the seedlings she set out from the pots that littered the windowsills of her front porch each spring. The late frosts killed some of them right away, the early frosts killed others in late summer, and in the hottest months the mid-summer frosts killed still others. And those few saplings that survived died during the winter, despite the piles of leaves Gladys heaped around them. Eventually almost all of them ended up in the huge, stinking compost heap she kept at the bottom of her garden. She put so many things in that compost heap that it would sometimes stay active all year, and more than once I saw, in the dead of winter, small plumes of steam percolating up through the snow.

Nothing exotic lived long in her garden, except for one small fruit tree. It had been planted before I could remember, and each spring it flowered profusely, and the white blossoms were succeeded in turn by masses of poisonous blue-black plums no bigger than cherries, and as hard as rocks.

Every kid in the neighbourhood knew the plums were poisonous. There were stories about those who had tasted them years ago, and how they'd sickened and died, or been sent away to the loony bin where they were said to languish still, dull, drooling and idiotic. Notwithstanding, Gladys never got to harvest her poisonous plums. Partly to make sure she wouldn't use them against us in some evil spell, and partly in the pure spirit of gleeful juvenile vandalism, each autumn one group of kids or another always succeeded in stripping the tree. The climate was too cold for horse chestnuts, and we needed something moderately lethal to throw at one another during harvest time. The plums were ideal. It was probably the reason Gladys seemed to hate us all so much—for weeks after the tree was stripped she was even more grumpy than usual, staring me in the eye for long seconds when I collected for the newspaper, no doubt having decided I was the villain. But she never came right out and accused me of anything, even though a few times I'd been among the culprits.

I don't remember the little tree growing much. Maybe we kids broke too many branches pulling the plums off, or maybe the tree grew taller as I grew and I didn't notice.

All of that was years ago. As soon as I grew large enough I left town. I hated that cold climate and I didn't want to die there, killed off like Gladys' exotic plants, or grown small and hard and poisonous like the plums.

I heard about her death while I was back there visiting friends. It seems that Gladys had a son nobody knew about until he came to live with her ten years ago. My friends had bought the house right next door to her place, and they had a ringside seat for what happened.

The son was nearly fifty, and he turned out to be a hopeless drunk. He couldn't keep a job, and he couldn't get along with anyone, least of all old Gladys. He'd come home dead drunk one night in the middle of a snowstorm, and Gladys threw him out of the house after an argument. He disappeared into the night and didn't come back. It snowed more than a foot that night, and the snowstorm continued unabated for several more days. After that, it turned bitterly cold. The snowpack was deep that year, more than six feet, and after a desultory search, and a lot of matter-of-fact tsk-

tsking and shaking of heads, people quickly lost interest in what had become of Gladys' son. It was cold, and most people assumed that he was either dead or that he'd left town on the bus the next day.

Well, he turned up right in Gladys' garden, underneath all her dead plants in the compost pile. It seems he'd burrowed his way under them, thinking, in his drunken stupor, to keep warm. They didn't find him until most of the snow had gone the next spring.

I heard all this while I was sitting on my friend's back porch, looking across into Gladys' garden.

"What happened to the old lady after that?" I asked my friend.

"Nothing much. She was pretty rickety by that time, and about the only change we noticed was that she started letting the garden go to hell."

I looked back into the garden. The plum tree was about fifteen feet tall now, and it was full of small blue-black plums.

"Crazy the way old Gladys gardened, eh?" I laughed. "The only thing that really worked in her whole garden was that plum tree, and all it ever produced were inedible plums."

"Those plums aren't inedible," my friend said mildly.

"Sure they are," I insisted. "We used to think they were poisonous."

My friend got out of his chair, leaped over the short fence into Gladys' overgrown yard and picked a half-dozen plums.

"We've been making jam out of them ever since Gladys stopped gardening," he said. "She told us to take them. As a matter of fact you had some of the jam at breakfast."

He tossed a plum across the fence. I caught it and rolled it around in my hand. It was no bigger than I remembered, but much softer. Then I bit into it, and let the nectar of the sweetest plum I've ever tasted roll across my tongue and into my throat.

Working Together

I worked on a union job once. I was twenty years old and there was big money to be made on the megaproject dam the Government was building up north and I wanted some of that big money and I wanted to see what it was like up there and maybe I wanted to buy a Camaro and drive it around real fast and loud and pick up girls so I could spend the big money I was making.

In those days it was easy to get one of those jobs. All I had to do was walk into the employment office and tell the woman at the counter I was willing to go up to the dam.

"Okay," she barked. "Sign here and be at the seaplane base tomorrow at 8:00 a.m. and they'll fly you in for free."

I didn't bother to ask what kind of work I'd be doing. I didn't have a trade so I knew I would be working as a labourer of some sort. That didn't worry me. I would work hard, and in no time at all I'd be on my way up. I asked, instead, about the wages, which I already knew were pretty good. With lots of overtime and the cheap room and board I'd get rich even if I didn't move up.

As I walked onto the rickety river dock the next morning along with five or six other men to board the twin-engined float plane, there was a matter-of-factness in the way the crew treated us that dispelled any sense of adventure we might have had. The way they untied the plane and then ordered us to put on our seatbelts let us know they did it every day, and it was no big deal that we were going up to the dam. They were getting paid, we were going to get paid, and most of the money would be drunk away in one bar or another. They'd seen all of us before, and would see all of us again before too long.

It wasn't until the plane was actually bouncing down the river on its takeoff that I realized I was going to a very strange place to do strange work and that, for the first time in my life, everyone would be a stranger. I looked around me in the plane, and the faces I saw suddenly bore no resemblance to anything I'd known before. Several of them showed apprehension, and one swarthy middle-aged man was so terrified I could see his teeth chattering. Several others, on the other hand, seemed completely relaxed, and one was already nodding off. What I picked up on right away was that each man on the plane was, in his own way, uninterested in his travelling companions. I'd never encountered anything like it before, and I amused myself with it for a good part of the hour-long flight, imagining that I was flying, during wartime, with a commando unit behind enemy lines, sent in to blow the dam up instead of building it. We therefore did not want to know one another, because in this business, all intimacy ended either in death or destruction.

By the time we'd been in the air twenty minutes I'd imagined more about the abilities and the personality quirks of my fellow passengers than they could even hope to know about themselves. We would be working together, I told myself from inside the commando fantasy, and I alone had to know what they could and would do if the mission were to succeed.

But as the plane came in over the small town that served as a supply depot for the dam, I remembered that it was early fall, and that at some point in the near future, winter would come. And as the plane landed on the small river that bordered the town on one side, I remembered that the river would freeze. My ambitions began to pull in and shiver. The commando fantasy evaporated as the plane bounced along, noisily reversing its engines and turning slowly back upstream to dock. I was Nobody, and this was no mission. I was a labourer, and I didn't even know what that meant.

It meant, I quickly found out, that I *was* Nobody, bunking in building C-14 with Nobody, a Portuguese labourer named Mario who spoke very little English. Most of the English I was hearing was meaningless anyway, and I spent the first few days in a fog of my own insecurities, camp procedures, and the visible certainty of everyone around me. They all knew what they were doing, and why, and what they were going to do next, be it in the next few hours or at the next megaproject.

One of the first things I found out was what it was a labourer was supposed to do. A labourer was supposed to do nothing. If he failed at that, a labourer was supposed to do as little as possible.

I was clued in right away. Somebody told me to move some pipe from one pile to another. I tore into the pile, thinking that if I worked hard something good would happen to me. All I got was a pudgy hand on my shoulder and one of my fellow labourers telling me to take it easy.

"Don't break your ass," he advised. "You should be able to work that pile most of the day."

I slowed down for a few minutes, but by late morning I was again scrambling around like a monkey trying to finish the job. By early afternoon I was back at the foreman, smiling and looking for better work. He raised his eyebrows when I told him I was finished, and gave me some clamps to sort while he found something else for me to do.

I sorted the clamps back and forth with a now-stubborn diligence. I could see no purpose in what I was doing, and I didn't even know what the clamps were for. The foreman soon caught sight of the pace I was setting and walked over to my pile of clamps.

"There's some seven-inch pipe to be moved up top," he said, pointing vaguely out at the yard. "One of the Teamsters will be around in a minute with a truck to pick it up. Come back here when you're finished."

I could find only two five-foot lengths of pipe, so I went back into the foreman's shack to get clarification.

"That's the pipe," he said irritably.

"What do you need me for?" I asked. "Can't the guy with the truck load it himself?"

The foreman peered at me wearily. "Listen, kid. Teamsters drive trucks. Labourers lift pipes. This is a union job."

I started to say something, but he cut me off.

"You want to keep working on this site you gotta learn to do your job and let everyone else do theirs. That's the way it's set up and that's the way it's going to be. You just load the pipe on the truck, and then you hop in the truck and keep your mouth shut until you get to the top, and then you jump out and unload the pipe. Then you come back here. Got it?" His face softened a little. "It's crazy. But that's the way it is. Nobody wants to do anybody else out of a job, that's all. You'll get used to it."

I tried to get used to it, but it bothered me. The only kinds of jobs I'd had were jobs where you had work to do and not enough time to finish it in. Work was something you did so you could go home. This wasn't like that, but I couldn't put my finger on exactly how it was different. I wasn't even sure there was anything wrong with it, except that it made the day a lot longer than I was accustomed to.

I puzzled over it for a few nights in C-14 while my room-mate Mario muttered and snored in his sleep. As I got to know him better, he seemed like a nice sort of guy, and his English wasn't as bad as I thought. He spoke badly, but underneath that he understood well, and he read books every night, big hardcover books, most of them in English. He usually stayed in the room when he wasn't eating or working, and I assumed that was what everybody did. I hung around the room and read detective novels.

One night I asked him what he was reading.

"Karl Marx," he said in his careful broken English. "Good thing to read. I am a communist."

I wasn't delighted to be rooming with a communist, but I held my tongue and tried to listen. My understanding of economic theory was straightforward; if you worked your ass off and made the right kinds of deals, you'd make a lot of money sooner or later. The way I'd grown up that seemed to be all there was to it. It had worked for my father and for all his friends. For them, communists were guys who wanted to fly over top of us, bomb the shit out of us, steal our money and make us all eat gruel and wear overalls. But I'd already learned that on this job pretty well everything operated differently than I was used to, so I put a lid on my father's prejudices and listened.

"Capitalism means slavery for the workers," said Mario. "The capitalists make us work, and then they steal all the profits from our labour so they can sit around on their asses and do nothing."

That didn't jibe with what I knew. My father was a professed capitalist, and he'd been working his ass off seven days a week for as long as I could remember. I pointed this out to Mario, but he waved my objections aside saying that my father wasn't really a capitalist, just a petty something-or-other hamburger, a servant of the real capitalists. Then he ploughed on with my education, explaining the theory of surplus value for me. It took, he said, a certain part of a worker's day for the worker to produce goods equal to whatever it cost to feed, clothe and shelter him. But the rest of his labour that day created surplus value, which the capitalists steal, thus producing capital. What he said made logical sense, and it seemed unfair in an abstract sort of way. Yet at the back of my mind remained the image of my father and his fourteen-hour days, and I raised the point that some capitalists worked harder than anyone else.

"I told you that your father is not a capitalist!" said Mario, shouting down my quibble. "His capitalism is not correct and he is not a true capitalist!"

"What does a capitalist look like, then."

Mario embroidered a portrait for me. I was probably misinterpreting what he said, but I got a portrait of an overweight middle-aged man with a moustache, wearing a black suit and top hat, lying around a California swimming pool and drinking martinis and eating caviar. He was surrounded by beautiful but corrupt Playboy bunnies in skimpy bikinis and the parking lot was full of sinister black Cadillacs driven by beefy hired goons.

"So what's communism supposed to be?" I asked, not feeling very enlightened by what I'd just heard.

"Everybody is free," Mario grinned. "In communism, the workers own the means of production and they get all the profits. Nobody steals the fruit of their labour."

I'd always heard that you lived "under" communism, not "in" it.

"Is Russia free?" I asked, blandly.

A troubled expression crossed Mario's face, as if I'd asked the same wrong question others had. "Russia has only started," he told me. "The masses in Russia are very stupid and don't understand their own freedom. When they do, the state apparatus will wither away. . . ."

"The what?"

"The state apparatus," he said with a trace of uncertainty. "The government."

"Doesn't the government own everything in Russia?'

Mario got up from his bunk. "No," he shouted. "It belongs to the people. I can't talk to you any more tonight. Ask me about it later."

He left the room and slammed the door. I could hear him halfway down the hall, cursing in Portuguese.

•

What Mario was saying sounded true in a general sort of way. I was having trouble fitting it to the specifics of what I already knew about economics. But I was having even more difficulty putting it together with this job. By Mario's logic, we were supposedly building a dam, which everybody would own, and everybody would benefit from. It seemed to me, therefore, that we should be working as hard as we could in building this dam, because, after all, social justice will result from common ownership and an end to private property and private profits. But in fact, nobody was working hard. I brought this up the next night as soon as Mario became visibly bored with the book he was reading.

"You believe in common ownership, right?"

Mario nodded.

"The government should be building this dam, right?"

He nodded again, a little less vigorously.

"Then why are we all fucking the dog?"

Mario looked bewildered until I realized he didn't understand what I'd meant. When I explained what the metaphor meant, he exploded.

For the first and only time in my life, I understood Portuguese perfectly. Then he began to intersperse it with phrases of English, and eventually, it was all English.

"You are a lackey! We do not work for the government here! We are working for the big companies. They take profit from our labour, and it makes no difference what the labour is and who pays for it."

"Okay," I said humbly.

"What we do here is reverse the business on the capitalists. We are not letting them steal the surplus value from our labour. The more labour we make, the more wages the workers produce. That way the capitalists do not get it."

"I thought what we were supposed to get is control over the means of production."

"Well," he said, looking a little doubtful, "that isn't as easy as it looks. The capitalists are very powerful, and in fact they own the government. We do not want violence, and so we wait. And we chip away at their power, bit by bit."

I was getting more confused by the minute. I kept on circling around the questions until Mario got irritable again and stomped out.

I learned several more contradictory things from Mario in the next few days. I learned that the division of labour was the capitalists' way of confusing us so we would be unable to recognize and seize the means of production or to understand the productive process. The workers, in turn, were combatting that by insisting on the strict division of trades in order to protect job security and prevent the companies from hiring untrained scabs at lower wages. And, I deduced by myself, the union's strategy was to create more labour, and more wages, thereby cutting the capitalists' profits. When I argued this to Mario, he merely said that I hadn't gotten it right, and that the unions were anti-communist, which I took to mean that they were in favour of capitalism and were practising a kind of reversed version of it, in which the goal was to produce wages instead of capital.

But the more I learned from Mario, the more confused I got on the job site. I responded the only way I knew how: by working harder. But the harder I worked, the more trouble I got into with the foreman and the shop steward. The jobs I got also grew progressively nastier. Within a week, I hit bottom—cleaning out huge vats used to mix the sealing cement they were pumping into the walls of the dam reservoir. I was given a scraper and a steel brush and told to spend at least a day cleaning each vat.

I hated the vats. They were dusty and claustrophobic, and since it was Indian summer, as each sunny day wore on the vat I was working inside turned into a huge cooking pot, with me as the item being cooked. The first two days I finished cleaning my vat before noon, and the foreman promptly stuck me in another. I already had a reputation as the filthiest man on the jobsite, and I was treated like a leper by my fellow workers on the bus back to camp. They seemed to consider it a matter of pride to remain neat and tidy throughout the working day.

On the third day I took a detective novel and spent the afternoon trying to read it. I couldn't concentrate, and instead I sat at the bottom of the scrubbed vat, sulking until the whistle marked the end of the day. On the fifth day I complained to Mario.

"Very easy," he said. "I have a friend in the carpenters' union. Fernando. He can get you a job as a carpenter's helper. Maybe you can work with me."

I stayed in the vats for two more days. On the morning of the eighth day, the foreman slammed the side of the vat with a sledgehammer and called me out.

He pointed at a small middle-aged man, the same one who'd been so terrified of flying on the way up.

"There's a Spic over there who says he wants you as a helper. You interested?"

"Sure. You think I like it in those vats? Only a nut-case would stay in there if he had a choice."

The foreman peered at me carefully. Until this moment, I think he thought I was, at very best, an idiot.

"You arranged this? How'd you get in tight with the Spics?"

"I room with one of them. They're nice guys."

"What's the price?" he leered. "You spreadin' for them?"

"Am I what?"

The look on my face convinced him I didn't know what he was talking about.

"What do you know about those Spic bastards?" he said, his tone becoming fatherly.

"Nothing. They seem okay to me."

About all I really knew about them was that Mario was a communist, and that didn't strike me as something you chatted about with your foreman.

"Listen," he said. "They're not much better than scabs. They all come over here just to make money. They stay for a year or so and then go back home with a bundle and have more kids."

"Sounds okay to me."

"Yeah, well, you get those Latin bastards without any tail for a year and they get horny, so watch it. You get in with them you better get a lock for your undershorts or they'll be inside them."

"Aw, come on," I said.

I didn't believe him, even though the metaphor disturbed me. What bothered me more was the venom with which he'd said it. He went on to explain how Fernando and his friends were stealing jobs and wages from qualified Canadian workers, and how they didn't drop shit-all in the camp poker games, which I decided then and there was his main interest in life and in me, because he asked me to drop over to his cabin if I wanted a game. I told him I might just do that, maybe later. All through the conversation the little guy had been standing there looking increasingly disgruntled.

•

Sure enough, he turned out to be the famous Fernando. And the first thing he told me was that I was going to be working with him, not with Mario.

"That son-o-beetch does that to me every time," he told me by way of introduction. "Some day I will fix him properly. You're going to be working with me building scaffolds. You afraid of heights?"

I was scared shitless of heights but I wasn't going to say anything about it. It couldn't be worse than the vats, and being a carpenter's helper was a definite step up, even if the wages weren't better. First, I would get out of the vats. Second, I would be able to use tools, something not permitted an ordinary labourer because using tools violated the sanctity of whatever trade was involved. I didn't know a thing about carpentry, but it didn't matter. I would learn, and I was eager to get to work using Fernando's tools, even if the most I was actually supposed to do was to hand them to him.

I was quickly set straight on that count. I was, it turned out, allowed the use of one tool, as per the contract. We were building scaffolds along the sides of the dam's reservoir, and my tool was to be a ten-inch crescent wrench; my job was to tighten or loosen bolts, depending on whether we were putting scaffolds up or tearing them down.

Fernando thought of his helpers as monkeys, and he expected them to be more monkey than carpenter. And for good reason. Whatever fears I had about heights were nothing compared to Fernando's. His performance on the plane had been no act. Fernando started getting nervous three feet up and grew worse the higher he went. Above fifteen feet he became deathly pale, and was utterly unwilling to go higher than about thirty feet. Since the scaffolds sometimes went as high as sixty feet, his helpers built the upper portions while he yelled instructions from below, tightening the lower bolts and building elaborate braces, the intricacies of which would have thrilled most engineers. For the first twenty feet, cement trucks could have been driven onto Fernando's scaffolds. But anywhere above forty feet, it was touch and go, and don't stand near the edges.

Unlike Mario, Fernando was no political philosopher. He liked to talk as much as Mario did, but the subjects he was interested in were never abstract. For him, the ingredients of reality were materials and tools—he could, for instance, talk for hours about the relative merits of different brands of crescent wrenches. He also complained loudly and more or less continuously about the sons-o-beetches who had put him in charge of building scaffolds—he thought they were punishing him for something. Sometimes he thought it was for being Portuguese, and, when he was feeling good, he believed they were picking on him because he was the best carpenter in camp.

The truth was that his skills were being wasted. In Portugal, Mario said, he'd been a master carpenter—a builder of fine furniture. And if the elaborate braces he built were any indication of the quality and ingenuity of his work, even I was capable of recognizing that he was good.

He hated everything about camp life: the trailers, the food, the lack of anything worth doing—which for him meant building things out of good wood. Good materials. When he wasn't on the dam site he was either eating the hated camp food in monumental quantities or sleeping twelve hours a night in the trailers he hated because, as he pointed out, there was not a single piece of decent wood in them.

He loved food almost as much as he loved good wood. The reason he'd been on the plane with me was because he'd flown out to buy what he called proper food—olives, sausage, canned peppers and whatever else he could find at the few delicatessens he had found in the city. His lunchbucket was always full of strange things I dutifully sampled and disliked nearly as much as he did the camp food.

Mario spoke of him reverently, telling me what a great privilege it was for me to be able to work for him. Somewhere in Mario's mind, I think, was a notion that communism was for people like Fernando. I didn't know what to think. There seemed to be an abstract and a real capitalism, and an abstract and a real communism, and then there was this place, the dam site, where all of those things were supposed to be at work. But mostly it seemed like none of us was really working all that hard. It seemed like the machines did all the work, and we tried to slow them down. And there was something else going on too, but I couldn't quite place my finger on what it was.

I tried my best to cover for Fernando, but my own fear of heights made it difficult. I began to use a lot of tools I wasn't supposed to, and the shop steward from the carpenters' union began to watch me like a hawk. He cornered me in the dining hall one afternoon when our shift was over.

"Listen, kid," he said in a voice that oozed self-importance, "I been watching what you're doing for that fucking Spic. You've been breaking a lot of rules."

"I'm trying to do my job," I said carefully. Fernando and Mario were approaching behind the shop steward, and I could see a scene shaping up. I wasn't going to admit to the real reason I was working the way I was. So far, the only people in the entire camp who'd been on the level with me were Mario and Fernando.

"Why can't you just fuck off and leave me alone?" I asked, rhetorically.

"Because you're encroaching on job privileges reserved for carpenters. It's all in the master contract. Nothing personal."

By now Mario and Fernando were standing right behind him, grinning at me.

"Besides," he went on, a sneer beginning to twist his ugly face, "you're only covering that fucking Spic's ass."

"Which Spic do you talk about?" Mario said in an even voice, from behind him.

The steward wheeled around and found himself staring at two angry members of his own union.

"Any of you assholes you want to choose," he said, realizing he was caught, but deciding to brazen it out. He poked his finger into Fernando's fleshy chest. "You, you lazy sonofabitch. I'm going to get you off this job site. You're nothing but a fucking D.P. fake." He spun around and pointed at me. "And you, punk, you're going down with him."

Before any of us could think of something to say he stormed out the door.

Mario wanted to chase him, but Fernando stopped him, saying that it didn't matter.

"Listen," he laughed. "Now the bugger will be too scared to come back tonight. He'll miss his dinner and it will serve him right."

For Fernando, that was revenge enough.

•

As I crawled across the shaky scaffolds during the next few days, I returned to the fantasy I'd had on the plane coming in. Each drill-hole I found in the rock face would soon have a hose pushed into it and concrete pumped inside to fill the imperfections of the cliff-face, but instead I placed in each an imaginary charge of dynamite. The sense of adventure I'd begun with, however, had now changed to a sense of injustice, fired by a combination of paranoia and hostility.

I tried to explain my feelings to Mario.

"You're probably right," he said without hesitating. "You might not get through the probation period."

This was the first I'd heard about a probation period. The company had one, he said, and so did the union. I was in danger, according to Mario, from both sides. Then he told me some other things I didn't know about, which affected me more than any of his talk about communism or capitalism.

Above the dam was a huge valley full of virgin timber. Because it was so isolated, the valley had been, previous to the start on the dam, more or less untouched. It was full of moose and grizzly, a kind of unannounced wildlife preserve. When the dam was finished, the valley would become a lake that would stretch 250 miles. Mario had heard some rumours about what would happen—both in camp and from his political friends outside.

When the dam had been announced, the government had said that the area to be flooded was a wasteland, with few resources other than some undersized timber. The new lake, they said, would become a "valuable public asset"—useful for booming timber to new mills, and a wonderful recreational area. I remembered my father crowing about it to his friends, how the new industry would provide jobs and new customers, and how the lake would bring tourists.

What Mario heard was more or less the opposite. The timber in the valley, he said, was prime, and the government had deliberately underestimated its extent. He also said that about 5000 moose would drown when the valley was filled, and that the government would have to spend millions pulling debris from the lake. The lake, because of the size of the trees in the valley, would never be useful for recreation; the bottom would remain unstable because of the big trees. There were even rumours to the effect that the enormous extent of the lake would change the climate of the whole area.

I didn't *want* to believe him about this any more than I wanted to believe what he'd said about communism, but I had to admit to myself that I was beginning to think he was right. This part of it made sense, just like a lot of the other things he was saying were beginning to make sense. I just didn't believe the stories I'd grown up with anymore, not the bullshit from the government nor the folksy slogans and homilies I'd taken for granted while I was growing up around my father's business. They all said the same thing: if we all work together and stick together, things will get better for everyone, and we will progress into a future full of sunny days and mechanical gadgets.

Now I was hearing the secret whispers that went on just beneath the surface, contradicting it: 'Every man for himself', the whispering said, and 'Dog eat dog'. What it boiled down to in my case was that I wasn't going to be allowed to work. I wasn't mean enough, and maybe I wasn't tough enough. Without thinking about why, I began to look for things to steal and for things to destroy. I stole some food and I looked for tools, but the only tools I could have stolen easily belonged to Mario and Fernando, and they were the only friends I had. I accumulated a fairly large stock of food in my room, but most of it either went bad or was gobbled up by Fernando, who had taken to visiting Mario and me in the evening. And there aren't a hell of a lot of things to break on a dam site.

As the days got colder, I fixed on the idea of pulling one big scam in which I would outwit everyone and then make a break for it, but I soon discovered that there was nothing in the camp that allowed you to use your wits, except maybe the camp poker game. I watched that for a couple of nights—saw the large sums of money the sharks were picking from the suckers, and decided that I wasn't going to scam anyone. I couldn't see any way to get at anything.

About a week later, Fernando and I were building scaffolds on top of a ridge that ran about seventy feet above the floor of the dam. The ridge we were building on was only a few feet wide, and beneath it a steep but smooth concrete slope ran to the dam floor. I could walk up the slope, but just barely.

On what seemed sure to be the last sunny day of the year, I was lying on my back beneath the grounding scaffolds tightening some bolts when my crescent wrench slipped off a bolt and hit my glasses, shattering the left lens. The lens was made of safety glass, and it remained intact: a lattice of crystallized particles. I took off the glasses, stared at the shattered web, and began to laugh. Without thinking, I rolled over to get up, and rolled right off the ridge and down the seventy feet of slope to the floor of the dam.

Fernando scrambled down the slope after me, thinking I was hurt, and a few curious co-workers came over, hoping something interesting had happened. I was fine, and I was still laughing. Fernando pulled me to my feet, and I showed him the glasses, and he started laughing too. We stood there like that until the foreman came up and told us to get our asses up the slope and get to work.

"I can't see properly," I said, pointing to the glasses in my hand.

He stared at them for a moment, as if deciding whether or not I'd done it on purpose, calculating the legalities of the situation.

"Tough luck," he said, finally. "There's nowhere you can replace them around here."

Fernando stopped laughing. "You can work anyway," he said, as much a question as a statement.

I said I'd try, and he helped me back up the slope as if I were a blind man.

I tried to work, but couldn't. I blundered off the scaffolding and down the slope several more times that day, and after the shift was over I went to the company office and told them I'd have to fly out to get some new specs.

The supervisor wasn't any more sympathetic than the foreman had been. "You'll have to quit," he said brusquely. "Seems the foreman ain't too fond of you, and neither is the shop steward." He looked up at me without real interest and added, "So I wouldn't reapply to come back."

He got out my file and put an "X" at the top of it. "You'll have to pay for your flight out," he said. "We'll deduct it from your cheque. There's a flight out tomorrow morning. You can get down to the dock by yourself."

I squinted at him through my shattered lens and tried to think of something eloquent to say that would demonstrate the contempt I felt for him and all he represented. But I couldn't think of anything, so I asked him when my cheque would be ready.

"Pick it up in the morning," he said, without looking up.

•

I trudged back to building C-14 to pack up. Mario said it was a dirty deal and that he was sad to see me go, adding that he'd enjoyed having somebody to practise his English on. Then he went over to the company office to see if Fernando could be transferred into the room we'd shared. He didn't come back after supper, so I spent my last night in camp reading a detective novel. I'd read it before, but knowing what was going to happen was sort of comforting. I fell asleep early, and slept a delicious, dream-filled sleep that had nothing to do with working on the dam.

I awoke at the sound of Mario closing the door to go to work. I got up, dressed, shouldered my knapsack and walked out of camp. On the road to the depot I noticed that most of the trees were bare. It was sunny and cold, and when the weather broke it would almost certainly snow.

There were five or six other men waiting at the dock when I got there, most of them joking and happy. Several of them gave me curious glances. I guess I looked pretty funny with the shattered lens on my glasses. I took them off, stuffed them into the pocket of my jacket, and climbed onto the plane. I settled into my seat and looked out the window, but the world was fuzzy, so I took out the detective novel, brought it close enough to my eyes that I could see the words, and began to read.

The Brotherhood of Men

Bobo phones, to ask how to play pinochle. It's about the fourth time he's asked, but it's easy enough to explain it to him again. I tell him what he's forgotten, and after some small talk about getting together soon, I hang up, smiling. Things weren't always as easy as this fraternal domesticity we share now that we're each living in a big city and have jobs and marriages to keep us busy. When I see him I still feel a twinge of fear because of his size, his bearing. Bobo is a large man who walks on his toes and waddles, and one of these days he'll be fat and bald.

But I don't think about that. I think about elbows and knees, about faces and broken teeth. This is because Bobo owns my teeth.

•

Bobo and I are different kinds of men. I've always been skinny and a yapper, and Bobo was, I suspect, over six feet tall at birth, and has never really needed to talk to anyone. The other main difference between us used to be more important than it is these days. Most people who know Bobo would tell you that he's a nice person. He's always gotten along with his friends and family, modelling himself after his father, who was also a nice person.

The difference is that for a long time I couldn't get along with anyone, least of all my father. That no one but me thought I was nice didn't, however, faze me in the least—I was too busy talking to notice.

Bobo, for all his niceness, made it a point to remind me that everyone thought I was a loudmouth. He rarely made direct threats, but he had his way of letting me know I wasn't his favourite person: "Someday," he would smile down at me, "I might have to punch that smart mouth of yours closed."

I responded by staying out of his way as much as I could. That wasn't easy in a small town, but it was easier than keeping my mouth shut.

A fight between us, we both knew, would be a strictly non-title affair between a pretty good heavyweight and a very flimsy lightweight. Happily, Bobo possessed a clear sense of the order of such things. Whenever he did fight, he fought big men like himself, and won at times, lost at other times, having made a fair and silent account of himself. The only times I fought without being cornered were with my father and then I always made sure everyone within hearing distance knew what a villain he was.

One spring I left home after a fight with my father, moved into a small shack that belonged to one of his enemies, and began throwing parties so my friends would have an occasion to get drunk and I would have a forum for yapping. Bobo came to the parties, and one night he cornered me and told me once again he was going to have to punch my head in if I didn't stop badmouthing everybody. Particularly, he said, my father.

Until that moment I'd never seriously considered fighting with Bobo. But I began to think about it a lot, because Bobo began to bully me more actively, breaking into my shack at all hours of the day and night, driving his old car around inside my yard and generally making fun of my beatnik pretensions. He threw parties at my house, and brought some very large and unfriendly people around to, well, look down on me.

I retaliated as best I could. I got some concrete blocks and spaced them around the yard, but he collected them and piled them on my bed after one of them demolished the front bumper and one of the fenders of his car. When he took to using my bed as the dumping ground for his empty beer bottles I decided that I'd had enough—I was going to have it out with him.

The tactical problem I faced was that I couldn't beat him in a fair fight, and I wasn't about to risk using a tire-iron or a beer bottle, lest such measures failed and I became the victim of my own weapons. I fantasized about drugging him, but the only drug I knew about was the diluted marijuana I'd acquired during trips to the coast, and that stuff wasn't about to put anyone to sleep.

One night, at one of my—or his—parties, I stumbled onto the opportunity I'd been looking for. Get him drunk, I thought, and stay sober yourself, and even things out that way. Bobo got very drunk indeed, and without my help. I drank nothing, and cunningly smoked some of marijuana, thinking, in those early days of the Revolution, to sharpen my wits with it.

From my elevated consciousness I carefully observed Bobo's condition, and when he emptied an entire bottle of beer into his own lap without noticing, I deduced that he was drunk enough.

I poked him in a friendly sort of way. "Hey, let's go outside for a minute."

Bobo rolled off the chair onto the floor and leered at me. "Yah," he said. "Hah hah, what are we going to do? Have it OUT?"

"Hah hah," I said, helping him to his feet and then following him as he staggered out the door. I watched him wheel around the yard as if he were trying to navigate by the stars, and announced that it was no joke.

"I've taken enough of your crap," I snarled. "Let's get it over with right now, once and for all."

Bobo's eyes narrowed with alarming coherence. I saw glee in them, and then some vicious anger crept into the glee, and as I was pondering my enlarged perceptual capacities Bobo's utterly sober voice broke through.

"Okay, smart guy," he said "let's just do that. Let's have it out."

He took his coat off with exaggerated care, but I didn't try the standard trick of slugging him while it was halfway off. My plan was not to mix with him, but to work instead on his lack of coordination, playing the role of toreador, with him as the bull. In my condition of hyperawareness I was sure I would be able to dodge all his drunken charges, and whack him as he went by until I knocked him senseless.

I drew him out into the grassy yard where I had plenty of room to dodge and run. Sure enough, he charged wildly at me, and I stepped aside and creamed him: Olé! He stopped and turned, looking mildly puzzled, then charged again. Whack. Olé!

What fun, I thought.

The strategy worked fine for five or six passes. I marked him up a little; drew some blood cutting him over one of his eyes. But he didn't fall down when I hit him—as a matter of fact he didn't even slow down. I started to think about that, and I slowed down instead, and he began to see what I was doing. It began to dawn on me that I was going to get hit in this fight too, and while I was thinking about that he charged. His shoulder caught my hip and sent me flying backward through the air. I landed on my ass in the grass.

Bobo chased me and I tried to wriggle away, rolling around and kicking my legs in the air, trying to get up so I could make a run for it, thinking that the son of a bitch could kill me, and just as that thought reached cinemascope proportions I was uprooted by the pantleg and stood on my head. For just a moment I could see the stars below me. Then I was set back on my feet. KRANG went a fist off my forehead and I was seeing a lot more stars. Suddenly a face blocked them out (O Joyous Cosmos come back!) and then a fist, bigger than the cosmos, was hovering over my face.

"For Christ's sake," I squealed, "don't hit me, I give up, I can't take you, don't hit me!"

The fist stayed there. "I'm going to punch your teeth down your goddamn throat," he said in the loudest and deepest voice I'd ever heard.

"Please don't," I whined. I would have cried, but the terror of the thought of my teeth being smashed in was so physical I'd forgotten how.

"Please don't do it, man, don't do it," I pleaded. Oh God, I thought, and closed my eyes, wondering irrelevantly if I would see even more stars.

There were no stars. I heard sobs instead, and opened my eyes to the starry night and Bobo.

"I can't do it, goddamn it, I just can't." He stopped, and his voice cleared. "Get up."

He pulled me up, almost tenderly, and I got to my feet, stumbling around a little with sheer fright, not touching him and not knowing what to do or what to say.

"Uh, thanks, man," I said quietly.

I felt grateful and ridiculously aware of my teeth, making a mental note to brush them more often, maybe even get some of that floss my mother had been nagging me to use. I wanted suddenly to be drunk, and I wanted for the first time in my life to be part of the brotherhood of men. It didn't matter who that included, even my father.

We made our way to the door of the shack and pushed it open. No one inside had even noticed we'd been gone.

"What have YOU been doing?" someone said.

"Oh, nothing," I mumbled.

Bobo laughed. "He just cleaned up on me," he said.

"Like hell I did," I said, laughing too, and we poked each other affectionately.

My gratitude changed to pride when I realized that I'd fought him, and it was over. I stamped around the room, pulled off my torn shirt and felt the muscles moving beneath my skin. I imagined that all the beautiful women in the world were looking at them with wonder, and I felt my own wonder that I had this body, these teeth to run my tongue over, now and forever to feel this firmness beneath my feet.

•

I don't think much about the debt anymore. Bobo still owns my teeth, still knows more about the brotherhood and its rules than I'll ever be comfortable with. All I know is the rules for pinochle, and how to live in a city grown too big for brotherhood.

Getting Bonded

Winter was coming, and I was broke, so I got a job driving truck for one of the soft drink companies. So did Bud, and so did a little guy named Bobby Sondis, which isn't his real name. I can't remember his real name and neither can anyone else. I got the job because I was smart and knew the business, and because I was one of the franchise bottler's sons from upcountry. They thought, I guess, that I was doing it to learn the business, as they say, from the ground up. The truth was that I was confused about what to do with my life. Like most of my generation I didn't know where the ground was or even what it was. I just needed the money, and driving pop trucks was the only work I knew.

Bud got the job because he was an experienced driver-salesman, having worked in the industry on and off since he'd been a teenager. He'd worked for my father for a couple of years, and I liked him. He'd taught me, among other things, most of what I knew about driving trucks, and with less success, how to talk fast when I didn't know what I was doing.

On my first day on the job I was sent right into downtown Vancouver with an eight-pallet flat deck, a Ford cab-forward truck of a type I'd never driven before. I'd never even driven a car in a big city, actually, but I didn't say anything about that to the supervisor who assigned me to the route. He handed me an invoice book and gave me a big burly guy as a swamper. The swamper was several years older than I was, and luckily he knew the route.

I thought I knew the business, but it was a morning for surprises. The first thing I found out was that I was buying my load from the Company every morning, and the Company was going to buy the remains of the load back from me that night when I came in. I was therefore responsible for any thefts, breakage or mistakes in between. The commission was ten cents for every full case I sold, and five cents for every case of empties I brought back, and I was getting a $60 a week basic wage in case my commission didn't turn out to be more than that.

I looked through the route sheets, and it didn't take me long to figure out I would have trouble making more than the basic wage. On a really good summer day, the route sheets said, I might sell 150-200 cases. That meant I would make about $50 a day, which in those days was reasonably good money.

But this was November, and a good day was about sixty cases, which might mean $20-25 a day, and if you dropped a few cases on the street it would come out to considerably less. The swamper told me I'd have to work about the same hours as in the summer, which meant I was getting lousy pay for the hours I'd be working. It also explained why he didn't mind being my swamper— he was making more than I was.

I learned some other things in the first few hours I was on the job. I noticed that the invoices weren't numbered. In my experience they'd always been numbered, and a lost invoice book could put you in deep trouble, because no one knew who you'd sold to, or how much. It prevented you from stealing from the customers, and it made it hard to steal from the Company unless you were in cahoots with one of your customers. Here, the invoices could go anywhere, but because you bought and cashed in your load every day, it was nearly impossible to steal from the Company. So, I figured, given the lousy pay, you were supposed to steal from your customers.

The second thing I learned that day was more disturbing. Halfway through the morning I was intercepted by one of the

Company's sales supervisors. He'd come to show me all the things I was doing wrong and to deliver, on the job, the Company Speech. He informed me, after some bullshit about how it was important to please the customers and to work hard, that it was important above all to be honest. I was, he announced proudly, going to Get Bonded.

I had an idea of what that meant. A bonded driver-salesman is one who is certified by an insurance company as fully capable of handling monetary transactions honestly and skillfully. The main reason for doing it is cosmetic. The Company is assuring customers that the Company is a "good" company that hires trustworthy employees. From a driver's point of view it means that if you screw up, you can never be bonded again, and you can't get jobs in a large sector of the service industry.

I had a problem. First, I wasn't going to be making enough to live on. Second, I was going to get bonded at the same time as I was going to have to steal to make a living wage. I mulled it over for a few days and made my decision. There was no point in whining about it. I'd have to steal.

Grafting, as it was called, was easy to learn. The techniques were simple. You took fifteen cases into a supermarket, got the invariably stupid bagboys to check it in, and then you hauled five of them back out and threw them on the truck. Another method was to use empty cases in between and under the full ones. The bagboys never checked to see if the cases you were bringing in were full.

Once you got your graft cases, you sold them to customers who paid cash—usually Chinese grocers. If you grafted ten to fifteen cases a day, you could make a living wage. If you got ambitious, you could make good money. Most of my fellow driver-salesmen, I soon discovered, were very ambitious.

After the first day I was given a route of my own in the east end of the city. It wasn't a good route—most of my customers were small grocers—so I had to steal the few supermarkets on the route blind. After a while there was a certain degree of risk involved. Within a few months, it seemed to me, even an idiot would be able to see what was going on. Officially, at least, I was selling large volumes to the supermarkets, and almost nothing to the small grocers.

Bud got a better route out in the suburbs with better volumes and better opportunities to graft. But he pointed out, when I complained that I felt like a sitting duck, that all the other routes looked the same from the Company's point of view, and that the Company knew what was going on anyway. It was, he said, better than paying people decent wages. Bud just shrugged when I said they were a bunch of assholes for turning us into criminals.

"That's the way things are," he told me. "You're the asshole if you think it's going to be any different."

•

On his third day at work, Bobby Sondis went around a corner too fast, and half his load went off the side of the truck. By the time he got the mess cleaned up, it had cost him $50. The Company let that one go, but his first paycheque was $36. He dropped his load again before he figured out how to make his truck go around a corner, and he went home the second week with $23. By the sixth week he'd gotten overconfident and did it again—this time right in front of the plant. I drove in ten minutes later, but I didn't stop to help. It was 7 p.m. and it was raining. So far, I knew, Bobby was averaging $40 a week.

Bud and I assumed he was grafting like everyone else. But one night he caught the downtown bus with us after work, and the first thing he asked us was how we made it on the lousy pay.

"It's not so hard," Bud smirked. "How much are you clearing?"

"I dunno. About forty bucks a week," he said.

"How much graft are you taking?" I asked.

Bobby seemed puzzled. "Graft? What are you talking about?"

"Graft," Bud said. "You know. Steal from the rich to get from the poor."

"You have to steal on this job," I said, "or it just isn't worth working."

"How do you manage to steal?" he asked. "The bastards check your load coming and going."

Bud rolled his eyes. "You don't steal from the Company," he said. "You hit the supermarkets and the other big customers, and then you sell what you get to your cash customers. Every driver in the place is doing it."

"That's dishonest," Bobby objected, his small eyes narrowing.

Bud and I started laughing. "What if you get caught?"

"Nobody gets caught unless they're totally stupid," I told him. "The Company knows we're doing it. That's why the wages are so low. It's no skin off their asses if we rip one guy off and sell it to somebody else. They still get their money."

The bewilderment in Bobby's face began to lighten into something like hope.

"Will you show me how to do it?" he asked, more of Bud than of me.

Bud nodded. The bus pulled up in front of the Biltmore Hotel and the three of us got off. It was 9 p.m. and we had cash in our pockets—at least Bud and I did. We were going to even things up by showing a working buddy how to score a decent wage, and it felt good.

"C'mon," I said. "I'll buy you a beer."

We got drunk, and Bud and I taught Bobby how to graft. He was a little slow to catch on, but even so, it didn't take very long. Later in the evening Bud told us some stories about the door-to-door bleach business he used to run. Then he told us he had 300 cases of Mission Orange stored in a friend's basement. That company had recently gone out of business, partly because their products tasted lousy, but partly because their drivers had been stealing them blind. A week or so before they folded, Bud had driven his truck over to his friend's place, and unloaded the entire truck. No one knew the difference, he said. I wondered if he'd been doing that to my father, but I didn't think about it too hard or for too long. Bobby's eyes were like saucers.

It wasn't that Bobby was stupid, and it wasn't what most people would call innocence. Bobby thought that when you worked hard you'd get paid a fair wage for it. Bud and I believed that maybe that was how things ought to be, but since we were confronted by an obvious exception to that rule, we didn't hesitate to act on the opportunity that exception provided. Whatever we believed about wage labour and "the system" was superceded by a much stronger conviction that the worst thing that could happen to a man was to be taken for a sucker. We also believed that if an opportunity presented itself, you were supposed to go for it, and the degree of restraint you exercised was pretty flexible. All that stuff about fairness and honesty was fine, but it was like thin ice. If the ice started cracking, you had to know what to do.

I had some private ideas about never ripping off friends, but I never did know where Bud stood on those kinds of questions. Not knowing didn't bother me, but I never really turned my back on him. Bud never turned his back on anyone or anything, and he was proud of it.

Bobby, on the other hand, believed everything he'd learned as a kid about what's good or true. This, I guessed, was his first experience with the way the real world operated, and he wasn't enjoying it. He didn't enjoy what happened next, either.

•

Two days later, he grafted six cases from a supermarket on the second stop he made, and sold four of them to his next customer, a Chinese grocer a few blocks away. A Company supervisor nailed him for it as he got back into the truck with the $12 cash in his pocket. He was fired on the spot, and told there was a good chance he would be charged. I heard about it when I got back to the plant that night. I'd grafted nine cases myself that day.

The supervisor who'd caught him was sitting around the office, no doubt at the management's instruction, bragging about it. His main point seemed to be that Bobby was a lousy driver and a wimp, and that he therefore deserved to be canned. The Company, he said unctuously, had suspicions that he was grafting, and had been watching him.

"That sawed-off sonofabitch will never get bonded again," he smirked.

He'd told Bud privately that the Company had decided that the grafting was getting out of hand, and that they wanted to make an example of someone. He'd hinted that they'd hired Bobby more or less for that purpose.

"No use screwing up someone who could turn into a good driver-salesman," he'd said.

"What a bunch of dirty bastards," I said to Bud when he related the story to me.

Bud shrugged it off. "No use getting upset about it," he said.

"But it's kind of a piss-off that we were the guys who told him how to do it."

•

The Christmas season was coming, and that meant a big push in the industry to get the customers to load up on mixers. A special system was set up so that customers could stock up without paying for it until after the Christmas season was over. The Company held a sales meeting for the drivers, setting up quotas for each route. The quotas were ridiculously high, with small cash prizes for the first three drivers to reach 50, 75, and 100% of their quotas.

It was with these quotas that the Company made their first and maybe their only mistake. The quotas provided a unique opportunity for us to screw the Company. Theoretically, you could load your customers up as much as you wanted, and you could make good commissions doing it. But if you oversold, you had to haul it back out again in January, and there was a reverse commission.

There were two loopholes in the set-up. The first one was obvious. It naturally afforded unusual opportunities for graft. It was common custom that during the first two weeks of the customer-loading period there were no cash sales turned in to the Company. It was, I heard, tacitly acknowledged as a Christmas bonus. But Bud spotted another more lucrative and totally legal way of cashing in.

I was bitter about the way Bobby Sondis had been treated, and I didn't hide it very well, least of all from Bud. I threatened to quit, and it must have been one of my tirades about quitting that tipped him off. On the bus going to work one morning early into the season he asked me if I was interested in screwing the Company, but good.

"Sure I am," I said.

"Well," he said, "then don't quit, and stop yapping about it."

I asked him why, and he grinned. "We're going to screw the Company on the level, and they won't be able to do a goddamn thing about it."

"Oh, sure," I said, sceptically, "I'd love that. How?"

"We're going to load our customers up until they've got mixers under their beds, and then we're going to quit and let the Company haul it all back. We get our commissions, and they won't be able to touch us. They'll have to pay someone overtime to do the hauling. We'll be screwing them double."

•

Four days later Bud hit 50% of his quota. He did it without turning in a single cash sale, and only one other driver had reached 25% of theirs. The other driver was me, and I was close to 40% of mine. Bud had 75% before anyone but me reached 40%, and he reached 100% by the time the rest got to half. Three days before Christmas he was close to doubling his quota. I'd reached mine and was closing in on Bud. No other driver was close to us.

That night the Company threw a party in the back of the plant, and treated us all to cheap rye in paper cups. Bud and I collected our bonus money and our commission cheques, and drank their cheap rye. The supervisors were ecstatic over our performance, even though one of the other drivers was upset because Bud had been servicing customers on his route. Bud was leaving for San Francisco the next day, but I was the only one who knew. I had a bus ticket to go home in my pocket, and even Bud didn't know that. We grinned a lot, drank our rye and said nothing. We were ready to leave when the regional manager showed up.

He was one of those people who talk in capital letters. "Everybody Hold On for a Few Minutes here," he yelled. "We have Some Door Prizes here for our Top Achievers."

I was about to walk out, but Bud stopped me. As far as he was concerned it was another opportunity, and he wasn't about to let us pass it up.

"Can We have our Big Three over here, Puleeaase."

Bud, the other winning driver and I shuffled over to where Capital Letters had set himself up. He was actually standing on a pop case. He was a short man, but he didn't remind me much of Bobby Sondis. I wondered what Bobby was doing at that moment.

"If you Gentlemen will Step around the Corner, you'll Find your Door Prizes Waiting for you," he said, moving his arms and body as if he was the M.C. on a T.V. game show.

Behind several pallets of empty bottles were three doors, each with a wire rack attached to it. The racks held a roll of toilet paper.

Each door had a name on it, and we dutifully went over and picked up our doors and walked back out to the jeers and laughter of the losers. Capital Letters was grinning broadly, and he shook hands with each of us.

"Seriously, Men, I want you to know that the Company is Proud of You," he said to everyone and to no one, "Merry Christmas and Use these Well. They might be the Doors to Success."

I was going to tell him what he could do with his door prize and his job and his phoney glad-handing good cheer, but Bud grabbed my arm.

"Let it go," he said quietly. "He's a jerk, and we're getting out of here. It ain't going to change. Let's just take what they gave us and go."

•

A few minutes later we were walking to the bus stop outside the plant, waiting for the last bus we would catch to or from anywhere near that place. We'd each left a note in the supervisor's mailbox with our name and a simple message: 'I quit'.

I never got bonded again so I don't know if the Company tried to do anything about the way we screwed them. Probably they did nothing. I don't know what became of Bud because I never saw him again. I don't know what happened to Bobby Sondis either. The Company closed the plant some years ago because the employees unionized. I remember thinking the next day on the bus back north that it didn't feel very much like Christmas, and that the small bond of trust I had with the way things were was broken forever.

Walpurgis Night

In the early 1960s I rented a small apartment overlooking the city I'd always wanted to live in, bought myself a typewriter, a bottle of Scotch and a small record player and settled in to start a career as a writer. The apartment was the second floor of an old house and had no private entrance, so anybody who wanted to see me being a writer after 10 p.m. had to throw stones at my window and steal a ladder or something similarly reserved for the romantically inclined, unless they were willing to brave my decrepit and slightly crazy German landlady.

It was the last night in April. I'd spent most of the day walking around the city looking for things to write about, and I'd done fine. The year was new, the city large and mysterious, and it was filled with exciting spots and exotic people. I'd made a jumble of notes: a list of flowers I'd been able to identify, a description of a car accident, possible titles for novels I wanted to write—*The Lonely One*, *The Dark One*, etc., all variations on the word 'one'. I'd even made a detailed description of an elderly derelict I'd followed at a distance through the downtown alleys, watching him poke through the trash-bins of a number of businesses.

It was around 9 p.m., and I was lying on the thin hide-a-bed mattress that served as both livingroom and bedroom furniture, smoking a French cigarette and practising how to drink Scotch straight without gagging. My notes didn't quite add up, and I was trying to figure out what to write down. I was about to give up for the day when a stone ping-ed against my window and I heard my best friend Jim hollering at the top of his voice from the street below. I hurried down the stairs and opened the door for him. Jim gave my glowering landlady a cursory Nazi salute and barged past me with a wild look in his eyes.

"I've written a play," he said. "I need you to read it."

Jim had come to live in the city about the same time I had, and for a similar reason. I wanted to write Great Novels, and he wanted to be the next William Shakespeare. He lived a few blocks away, and like me had a small apartment in the upper floors of an old house. He even had a crazy German landlady.

I poured two Coke glasses full of Scotch, handed him one, and sat down on the floor to read the typed sheets he'd given me. Despite his agitation, he sat down on the floor across from me and kept silent while I read. The only sounds in the room were the muffled strains of Wagner from downstairs (my landlady played Wagner's operas on her old record player sixteen hours a day) and gagging noises whenever one of us swallowed a mouthful of Scotch.

Jim's play was about some people who were trapped inside a New York subway car. There had been a power failure, the lights had gone off, and the subway system had clanked to a halt, trapping Jim's characters in the bowels of the city. The situation seemed oddly familiar despite the fact that neither Jim nor I had been to New York or seen what a subway looked like.

"Where'd you get all this stuff from," I asked, looking up at him curiously.

Jim looked away. "I don't know. I read about it somewhere, I guess. What does it matter?"

"I don't mean that you stole it," I said. "I'm just curious about how you know things like this."

"I thought it up," he said, annoyed. "It doesn't matter."

I shrugged. Maybe it did come from the books we were reading. We'd both, for instance, been reading the novels of Nathaniel West, and had devised from his work the principle that all literary activity should end in disaster, cataclysm or personal extinction. Since the world around us gave every indication that it planned to bring all three of those down on us any day, we saw every reason to think that what we wrote should emulate and predict that reality.

Jim's play certainly was consistent with that principle. Inside the darkened subway car his characters quickly began to argue and when they came to an impasse they fought, verbally at first, and eventually so violently that they began to kill one another. I was troubled because I couldn't see what it was they were fighting over, but that, of course, didn't matter. At the end of the play there was only one person left alive as a witness, and that character resembled the author.

"This is all crap," I said tactfully. "In the real world, you would have panicked first, but I don't think you'd have killed anyone."

Jim stared at me silently. I choked down a mouthful of Scotch and passed the summary judgement I thought I'd been asked for.

"The play," I said carefully, "has energy, but it's rather imitative. It's also goofy."

I'd learned to use the word "energy" from reading New York critics, who said that energy was a good thing in young writers. Unfortunately, the other two descriptive terms I'd used came from closer to home, and that's where they landed. Jim turned pale and stared out the window. Unfazed, I plunged on, telling him that if real people were trapped in a subway car, half of them would go to sleep, or play cards, and entropy would govern, not violence. Or, another way, the lights would have been out, and so half the people would have slept, and the rest would have whimpered and complained, and if one or two *had* panicked, a former Boy Scout (which I happened to be) would have put a stop to it. I crowned my outpouring of practical wisdom by pointing out that it's impossible to put on a play in more or less total darkness.

Jim told me where I could stick my criticisms, and got up to pour himself more Scotch. Maybe, I began to realize, I'd derived a slightly different message from our reading of Nathaniel West.

"I'm not so sure reality is that easy," I said. "If it doesn't work the way you want it to, you don't manufacture a disaster. Those things have to happen to you naturally. You can't go around making them up just because you want something interesting to happen. That's selling out."

"Who to?" Jim asked sullenly.

"I don't know," I admitted, wondering exactly what we had to sell and who might want to buy it. "You know what I mean."

"No, I don't," he said. "Nobody wants to know the truth and even if we knew it, they wouldn't buy us off to keep us from telling it."

"Would you sell out?" I asked, shocked.

Jim didn't answer. Instead, he leaned back against the wall and stared at the raindrops that had begun to slap gently at the window.

The two of us sat on the floor of my dingy apartment half listening to the muffled strains of Wagner filtering up from below us, talking, as we had many times before, about how to become Great Writers. But this night I seemed to be doing most of the talking, and something had gone wrong. I was suddenly unsure of what we really wanted to be. I didn't have a clue about what was in Jim's mind, except that they weren't the same things, apparently, that I had in my own teeming brain. We'd talked any number of times about selling our souls to the Devil and we'd talked about losing them because maybe we were just too stupid to keep our souls. But for me none of that counted–it was just talk. I didn't believe that there was a "Devil" to sell my soul to, and, deep down, I didn't even believe that human beings had souls. Instead, what I really believed in was the existence of stupidity: people got hit by cars, or got too drunk too often–things like that. If evil existed, it had no embodiment, and it didn't buy and sell. True Protestant that I was, evil was weakness and corruption, not what caused those things.

But at the same time as I didn't believe in the physical existence of evil, I carried around a very literal concept of Good. What was good in the world was neither God nor Power nor "Good Works". Good was Literature, and I surrounded myself with it, and with the models for conduct that spilled from it. To that point in our short careers, Jim and I were, as far as I was concerned, purely and beyond reproach, on the side of Good.

This concept of how the world worked had both an existential and a pragmatic base: neither of us believed we were going to get to live very long, but we believed that despite our personal fates, Literature would somehow survive the coming apocalypse. Because it was truly "Good", meaning it was altruistic, unselfish and relentlessly in pursuit of the Truth, Literature possessed an indestructible permanence that would survive our crazy world. As writers, we participated in that Goodness. So long as we pursued the goal of becoming Great Writers with an ineluctable purity, the world would be allowed to go on. Literature would protect it and us.

It wasn't logical, of course, and I never worked it out precisely; had I done so it would have collapsed on me. It was more of a feeling I had about the way things should be, and since the alternatives the real world presented for a future were demonstrably suicidal and insane, I clung to my theory of Literature-as-reality. I had assumed that Jim felt the same way I did.

As a writer, I only had notes so far, no Great Novels. I didn't seem to be able to get past page ten, and even at that I knew what I was writing was bad. I wasn't worried in the slightest by any of this. Literature was perfect, but what got written, particularly by Jim and me, didn't have to be. As the rain beat down harder on the window, I tried to explain to Jim that it was just fine to have written a lousy play, that it was, actually, exactly the kind of thing we were supposed to be doing.

Maybe I didn't explain it very clearly, or maybe Jim wasn't listening, but I didn't get through to him. Maybe it was the rainstorm blowing itself into a heavy thunderstorm that did it. Whatever it was, the lights abruptly went out, my landlady's Wagner opera was silenced downstairs, and Jim and I sat in my darkened apartment inexpertly sipping our Scotch, watching the storm slam and shake the city. For a moment, Jim's spirits seemed to lift, and he said it was a night for the making of witches' brew.

"That's nothing to celebrate," I said primly. "Tomorrow is the first of May. We should think about celebrating that."

"What the hell for?" he answered, morose again. "It's just another lousy day in another lousy year. All we'll have to do is try to write something else."

"I guess."

Out the window we could see that there were lights on in other parts of the city. Suddenly I hated being in the only part of it that was dark. "Let's at least go someplace where there are lights," I said.

"Let's go get drunk," he answered.

I couldn't think of anything else to do, so we put on our coats and walked through the darkened neighbourhood in the pouring rain to a bus stop, caught a downtown bus, and went to a bar.

Jim was still depressed about something, and I guessed it was about the play. I wasn't much help. He wanted it to be perfect, and as far as I was concerned, being perfect was neither a requirement nor even a desirable possibility. The more I thought about it, the more firmly I decided I was right. It was the only thing about writing I had thought through, and what I'd figured out didn't require or even allow that I be perfect for a long time to come. I'd gotten most of it, I guess, from the American critic Dwight MacDonald, who said that no writer in this culture could or should mature quickly. Unlike writers from the past, like, say Keats or Shelley, who grew up with a raft of social privileges and within a culture in which writers were accorded a kind of moral expertise that made it acceptable to work without being self-conscious about the social value of what they were doing, young writers today have to learn the structures and social techniques of the culture strictly as citizens. Jim and I, along with everyone else, had to learn our way through a plethora of social skills and technologies that have no direct relation to writing—from learning to defend oneself in a fist fight, to learning what women are and what they want, to driving cars and trucks, to using credit cards. It's a long list, it's still growing, and it isn't what this story is about.

No writer, MacDonald said, faced by so complex an array of non-literary demands, should expect his talent to mature before, say, the age of 35. That I thought of myself as fundamentally different from the people I saw on the streets every day doing the same sorts of things I was learning to do, seemed to be to be no impediment. I wanted to be the next Shelley, and it seemed to me that all the things I had to learn were giving me a way of becoming a better writer than even Shelley had been. It made being alive exciting yet safe, because everything I did was part of learning to write. It also gave me a comforting sense of abundant time, considering that I also thought the world might go up in a cloud of radioactive smoke at any moment.

I thought being a young writer was great fun, and I specialized, mostly by accident, in grandiose intellectual errors and solecisms of technique. I enjoyed it when Jim ripped the adjectives from my mushy chocolate prose, or told me that my poems were too twitchy and adolescent. It was all true, but I would get better someday. And meanwhile, I was helping the world to go on.

The drunker Jim and I got that night, the more we argued about all the things we'd agreed on before. The more bitter the argument got the more I stuck to my ideas about not having to be perfect, and the less I liked Jim's play. At last, it boiled itself down to a sticky tar.

"You can't write about crap you don't know anything about. If you don't know the story, don't make it up."

"I didn't make it up," Jim yelled. "I got it all out of another play, and you just haven't read it."

"Then it isn't your story," I yelled back. "It isn't the right one, because you don't know if it's true or not."

•

And there we were, dancing at the junction: Literature, Life, all of it. From there, no matter what we did, everything became uncertain, as if a mist suddenly filled the air, because this argument goes on forever.

This is not Shakespeare's time, and it is no longer a time when Great Novels can be believed. We can no longer confidently know what the truc story is, as writers and readers once could. We don't even know if there is a story. And typically, after years and years of thinking about it I'm not sure exactly what happened the night of my story.

If we look at what might happen next, these seem to be my alternatives:

1.) The two young men can get drunker; can talk, fight, or find love either by splendid chance, or, I suppose, with each other.

2.) Some catastrophe can happen to one or both.

3.) The story can stop now, having offered some possibilities of being, some speculations about the real world and about Literature, and you, the reader, can complete the narrative in your own way and draw your own conclusions, just like in those Encyclopedia Brown books they give to children nowadays.

4.) The story can discuss, as so much writing does these days, The

Apocalypse, which is to say, it can give up on the story, on Literature, and on the entire question of the real world and what it should consist of.

In one part of the story, shortly after that night, Jim gave up wanting to be the next William Shakespeare and chose The Apocalypse, and there is very little, as a consequence, that I can tell you with any authority about the years he's spent since then waiting for it. I know he tried to make it happen every day in small and depressing ways. Booze, drugs, rain-filled ditches, flophouses, jails, fist fights, empty highways in the middle of the night. It's the sort of stuff I would have found romantic then, but now I don't believe that's what the story is about.

That night, you see, we got much drunker and argued violently in the bar. We drank uncounted glasses of beer, and I wondered out loud, partly to distract Jim and partly for the sake of form, when the beautiful women we were told would be showered upon us would arrive to solve all of life's problems. Jim wasn't impressed with my speculations, and we continued to argue, obliquely, about who was selling his soul; and about how, where, and over what such a transaction might take place. I remember that at one point our conversation was drowned out when someone in the bar flipped a coin into the jukebox and it played one of the Wagner overtures. But I might be imagining this part of the story.

Eventually the bar closed and we walked across a long, wide bridge, and quite probably we *both* considered jumping. If I did think about it, I would have thought about how to survive the jump. Jim's thoughts were possibly more serious. We did not find love that night. We talked; I hoped for great Literature; and Jim hoped for nothing.

Here is another possible version: we didn't reach the other side of the bridge. A black 1956 Buick with a single headlamp suddenly careened across the empty traffic lanes toward us as we approached the crown of the bridge. It jumped the curb, knocked me fifty feet along the railing, and sent Jim flying out over the filthy waters of the inlet below. He was still carrying the play he'd written, and the sheets fluttered down to the water after him like huge, uselessly unique snowflakes. That would have been Jim's story if he'd hung around to write it.

I'm still trying to figure the story out. Life has gone on, even though something I cared a lot about ended for both of us then. The Apocalypse hasn't come, and it won't so long as I continue to work with the idea that a writer can't be a Great Writer until he knows his world with complete intimacy, and that the job of Literature is to keep the world going.

Jim is gone. He's somewhere inside his personal Apocalypse of the Stormy Night, dead drunk in a rooming house, acting as if he's met the Devil I have no way of believing in, hoping that everything I write is a lie.

And tomorrow, beyond him, beyond this argument, is May Day.

The Franz Kafka Memorial Room

It was a small room at the end of a corridor, rectangular in shape, with a high ceiling—perhaps twelve to fifteen feet. Three walls were made of concrete construction blocks, while the fourth wall, which opened into the corridor, was of steel and glass, and included double doors. Only one thing was in the room: a staircase, opposite the door, led eleven steps up to a blank wall.

The room was discovered one week after the institution it was part of opened, and within a few days, someone with a sense of humour stuck a neatly lettered sign on the door: The Franz Kafka Memorial Room.

The room, you might argue, can be explained. It is part of a "Long Range Plan", which is a device invented by bureaucratic intelligence to create the illusion of competence and control in the face of an economy accelerating more rapidly and massively than at any other time in history. I explained the room to myself that way at first. It was just part of the Long Range Plan, and in the next stage of construction, the blank wall at the top of the staircase was to become a doorway to another corridor.

These days, though, I'm not so sure about things like that. Are you? Can you make the assumption that we are in control with the same self-assurance people could a generation ago? What if I told you that the next stage of construction didn't take place, or was altered in such a way that the extension of that corridor deep into the bowels of the institution was never finished? What if I told you that the corridor, and the blank wall the staircase led to, was meant to be just that? What if I told you that somewhere in that institution the Franz Kafka Memorial Room still exists, with the sign removed from the door, the glass and steel replaced by more concrete construction blocks and a wooden door with a number painted on it—say, 2062? Inside the room, do the eleven steps of the staircase still end at the blank wall? Or did they jackhammer the staircase away to prevent it from having an invisible existence?

I can't give you the correct answer to those questions. No authority exists that can, and I'm convinced that such a condition of uncertainty is now the true one for me to be in as the writer of the story and for you as the reader.

But this is depressing theoretical stuff, you might be saying to yourself, and why lay it on me here, in what is supposed to be an occasion for fiction. I mean, what is this? A lecture or something?

It's no lecture. I'm trying to tell my story correctly, and I want to set you up to think carefully about what happens to stories when nothing in the world is going anywhere. What is *supposed* to happen in a story? What does narrative involve? How can I believably offer up a beginning, a middle, an end, along with all the usual paraphernalia of fiction—character development, progression of image and idea, cautionary moral, a downer to let you know this isn't propaganda for the Chamber of Commerce or something sweet and sentimental from the Bureau of Sleep?

•

One sunny morning last week I was sitting in the Cafe Italia trying to think my way through this story. I like the Cafe Italia. It's large and spacious, and most of the time Tony, the owner, fills it with the kind of music you hear in Fellini movies, the kind of music that makes you believe that life is a cheerful dance that drools significance. But on this particular morning Tony had tuned in an FM rock station, and the place was jammed with synthetic adrenalin instead. I could hear an aerobics/rock number by Olivia Newton-John called "Let's Get Physical", one that presents life and love as messy distractions that come up between the hours when the discos close down and the muscle parlours open up. And the tune was having at me, despite my attempts to close it out, when I spotted an elderly man crossing the street.

He was carrying a manila folder under his arm, and he had a bad leg that forced him to walk with an awkward hippity-hop. I watched him make his way across the street, thinking that the leg must be causing him some pain. Then I noticed that he had a wide grin on his face, and that he was hop-hobbling in perfect time to Olivia Newton-John.

I'd seen the old man before, and I began to remember the first time I'd seen him, twenty years ago when I was in high school. Tony brought over the cappuccino I'd ordered, noticed that I was watching the old man, and smiled.

"He's a writer too," he said. "Did you know that?"

I knew but pretended I didn't so I could hear Tony's story. He likes me hanging around, and in his shy European way he is proud of my presence, and occasionally even curious about what it is that I write in his cafe.

"Yes," Tony went on, "he's writing a book about World Government. He comes here every day, like you, and does some writing on it."

"I know him a little," I admitted. "A long time ago he came to my home town to teach in the school. He's an interesting man."

Tony nodded, not interested at all in *my* story. He knows the old man as a street character in a big-city Italian neighbourhood, and probably thought I was making my story up. The old man had lived in the neighbourhood for a long time, also running a coffee bar, where he'd conducted an informal and almost certainly illegal psychiatric practice. Everyone knew him, and most knew he'd written books on a variety of subjects. No one, including Tony, read his books, but that didn't diminish the offhand kind of respect with which he was treated. To them, as to me, he was Dr. X, from the University of Rome, subject and nature of doctorial expertise—obscure.

He appeared in my world one autumn to teach Health & Personal Development (a euphemism for social and sexual indoctrination) and drama at the high school. He was in his forties then, short and balding, and he spoke an articulate English under the liquid stutter of a heavy Italian accent. My HPD classes with him were different than any others I'd experienced. They consisted of long monologues concerning Familial Love and Duty and the Attractiveness of Romance as a Way of Living, the latter lessons illustrated frequently by equally long digressions about how much he loved his young and beautiful wife, who'd remained in Italy for reasons the Doctor easily convinced us were well beyond our understanding. I think, in retrospect, that he saw his job as one in which he was to provide us with a vision of how life was supposed to be, leaving the teaching of its detailed workings to the school of hard knocks, which was the one most of us were headed for.

His method of teaching drama was equally novel. In the very first class he announced that we were going to write a play of our own, and then perform it in front of the school. This was unheard of—like asking a teacher questions in Health and Personal Development class. There was to be no memorizing of tedious lines from incomprehensible Shakespeare tragedies, no examinations—in short, none of the conventional signposts by which we normally determined our place in the conservative cosmology of high school.

Nearly everyone, including most of his fellow teachers, quickly decided that the Doctor was crazy. But a few of my friends and I thought he was sensational. He carried around all kinds of exotic information, and he was a compulsive talker. We were his most appreciative audience in that small town, and after a few months, we were just about the only audience he had, aside from the local Women's Art Circle.

But the Doctor was neither nut nor screwball. Not at all. He was a much more unusual sort of human being. He was an expert on all varieties of credulity, and he taught my friends and I something about that limitless storehouse of human credulity, and how it can either be avoided or used to advantage. He taught us to pay attention to the way people chose small parts of reality to sustain themselves, and he taught us to pay equally close attention to the parts of reality those same people suppressed. But mostly he showed us how reality operated by being transparent in how he himself manipulated it. Exclusion, his teaching told us, is the truest trick of a charlatan. And, his teaching implied, exclusion is the most dangerous power of Science, Politics, and Art.

The Doctor never actually admitted that he was a professional charlatan. We recognized it only because he showed us that his identities were as multiple as his abilities. Shortly after he arrived in town he let it be known, for instance, that he was a painter and a psychologist. It was those two identities that brought him to the attention of the Women's Art Circle. Whether he discovered the Circle or the Circle discovered him will remain forever obscure, but he was soon at its centre. The town was short on Psychologists and Artists, just as it was short on everything but trees, trucks and money. The Doctor was from another world, and he played the role of the exotic to the hilt.

Nobody knew enough to be able to evaluate his competence. Only now, and only in the most protected circles, is the competence of Psychology and Psychiatry questioned, and then only in the abstract.

To be sure, a few wealthy loggers with wives in the Art Circle naturally made sure the Doctor's appointment by the school board would not be renewed, but that back-handed critique was predicated on simple jealousy.

Unfortunately, I don't know if the Doctor was a good painter or not. I saw some oil paintings of his that looked like copies of Salvador Dali's paintings, slithering wristwatches and all, but I couldn't say if they were prints, copies that the Doctor made of the originals, or approximations of the style. Precise data after twenty years isn't available.

What I do remember is the afternoon he showed us the landscaspe paintings he was selling to the women in the Art Circle in large quantities, and I remember how he painted them: with his fingers. Then I remember him showing us how, when he blocked off a portion of these finer-manufactured landscapes, they *looked* like finger paintings Then, as we watched, he took another of his paintings—also a landscape, but painted, he said, with brushes—and blocked off a portion of similar size. It looked to us like part of the whole painting.

"That's how you tell a good landscape painting," he said, "or any painting that's good. Any part of it can be recognized sensibly as part of its larger whole."

•

As an absolute tool for evaluating all painting, the Doctor's principle is faulty. But I still don't know if what he told us about representational painting is true or not. I've tried to find out, but no one seems to be able to confirm it one way or the other. Some of the authorities I've questioned—and there have been a few—just laughed at me, while others, more modestly, have admitted that they just don't know. The questions his casually offered principle raised in my non-painter's head do not, apparently, arise very often in the minds of the professional practitioners of the field. Few of them seem interested in landscape painting, preferring to leave it to the amateur Art Circles, amateur airplane pilots and to whoever (or whatever) paints those paintings that can be seen advertised on late night television, the ones that show up for sale in gas stations or vacant lots whenever the weather is pleasant. "Genuine Original Oil Paintings for under $49.95" say the signs, and lined up next to one another are five or six or fifty identical genuine original oil paintings. And people buy them, not because the paintings are "good" or "bad" but because they're there to buy, they're cheap, and there are more empty walls in the city than Salvador Dali could imagine in his most lascivious nightmare.

The Doctor stayed in my home town for just that one year. My friends and I enjoyed that year of our lives mainly because of him, and so, probably, did the members of the Women's Art Circle. Our drama class wrote an original play for him, which was about a migration of teenagers to the Planet Mars. When we performed it in front of the school, the other students thought it was funny in all the places where we meant it to be serious, and I contributed by forgetting most of my lines. The few teachers who attended the play left after ten minutes and drank coffee in the staff room. I never thought to ask myself if the play was recognizable as a sensible part of the rest of the world, and I'm pretty certain that not very many other people in town asked themselves questions like that. I don't think the Doctor enjoyed his year in my home town.

•

Twenty years later, here's the now-aged Doctor hobbling across the street with a half-written book on World Government under his arm, and I'm still wondering about his method of detecting bad landscape painting. He enters the Cafe Italia and sits down at the next table and orders a cappuccino.

He doesn't remember me, and I don't introducc myself. I've always assumed that he wanted to forget the episode in his career that I was part of, and for all my curiosity about people, I'm a reasonably considerate person. But he does look over at my table, sees my manuscript papers and my nearly empty cappuccino, and smiles at me. I grin back, and together, and in our separate ways, we go back to trying to figure out what it is that really is going on, and what to think and say about it.

•

Let me try another way. Last night I watched the news on television. There was a long and unusually lurid film clip of a car-bombing in Lebanon. The news story contained no unique or even unusual pictorial or analytical content: it offered nothing about who had done the killing and nothing about why people were dying, and it seemed almost smug about not knowing. It was interested in the ever-renewable novelty of blood and gore, and it took delight in recounting statistics about how many people had been killed, particularly the numbers of women and children.

As I watched the film, I saw a man pull a dead infant from the rubble, and then pass the body to another man who carried it aloft through a crowd of onlookers, its small dark head flopping back and forth. Some of the people in the crowd were mourning, but many appeared to cheer at the sight of the dead child. As he reached the thick centre of the crowd, the man the camera was focused on leaped up onto some rubble, still holding the corpse of the child aloft with one arm, and raised his free arm *in a gesture of victory*.

Then the program faded to a commercial for men's cologne: a handsome, bronzed American male lifted a six-foot cologne bottle over his head, turned to the camera and brought the bottle down, exposing the brand name. He did not then give the victory sign. That commercial was followed by another on behalf of the Beef Growers Association, depicting a variety of ways to prepare and eat meat. That in turn was succeeded by a crisp commercial for a franchise restaurant advertising steak and prawns, and implying that if I was really socially competent I would eat their food and participate in their lifestyle. The jingle was catchy, and the people who appeared in the commercial appeared to be extremely pleased about something. Finally, there was a fourth commercial, again advertising perfume, but this time for women.

I clicked off the television set at that point, having seen more than the newscast intended me to see, and realizing instantly that I'd seen the Doctor's recognition principle inside out. The first conclusion any sane person will draw from the sequence is that television has produced a new and toxic strain of vulgarity. It should be banned. But we already know that, and we watch television anyway, right?

What I would like to draw your attention to is not a moral issue, but a technical one: where does a story begin, what are its responsibilities to material and social existence, and where does the story end?

It *can* end with a bang. Those cold-eyed and fundamentally crazed logicians who run our governments—ours and theirs—*can* push those red buttons many of us have nightmares about. If they do, they'll do it out of sheer terror and frustration, because they don't want to live outside the insular body of professional procedure, and they must certainly be aware, like everyone else, that the body is decaying rapidly all around them. We all look alike these days, sad splendid animals that we are, hobbling up and down the indeterminate corridors of the Institution in perfect time to Olivia Newton-John with our singular memories and our ideas about World Government.

But what if the story *doesn't* end, and what if the present confusion is just signalling to us that we have to reinvent the story? Maybe you recall the Doctor's young and beautiful wife, the one who remained in Italy for reasons that were beyond the ken of me and my teen-aged friends. Did you find yourself wondering if she really existed, or if the Doctor just made her up?

At the time, a lot of people wondered. No one could figure out how such a beautiful young woman could love a short, fat, balding, middle-aged charlatan teaching drama, social behavior and sex education to loggers' kids in a small town, and mass-producing landscape paintings with his fingers. Even I doubted the existence of the Doctor's beloved wife, although he often showed us a rumpled snapshot of her that he carried in his wallet. But the woman in the snapshot—beautiful and white-blond-haired—could be, I thought, from anywhere. And anyway, Italian women don't have blond hair. I don't know what the women in the Art Circle believed, but I did find out, years later, that he showed the photograph to them too, although for what reasons, and to what effect, I've never discovered. Maybe he turned them all down because he loved her so much, or maybe he used the photo to convince them he was the finest lover in all the world.

I can verify, however, that the young woman in the photograph was the Doctor's wife. About ten years ago I saw them together on this same street, where he now hobbles around with his book on World Government. They were walking arm-in-arm, and she looked ten years older than her photograph, but she was, if anything, more beautiful. And if appearances mean anything, she and the Doctor were very much in love.

I know this isn't much to go on, and I don't even know where the Doctor's wife is now. I haven't seen them together for several years. But when I think of them together, and when I see him bumping across the street like the crippled butterfly he is, the world brightens, and the stinking colossus of doom that darkens everything these days dissolves, and the walls that enclose us open up to the story as it might be, whirling around and around in the air.

Shelley's Red Ink

Most people will tell you that the world gets smaller as you get older. But for me the world began as a small and orderly place, and since then has grown progressively larger and more untidy. And there is more than one world.

By the time I was eighteen I could see that there were at least two distinct worlds. One was the small town world I'd grown up in. It was, by turns, either dull or threatening, and often both at the same time. The other world, the one I was more interested in, was largely literary. I was ingesting vast quantities of characters and ideas from the books I was reading, and the characters were popping up all over town. French Existentialists drank sour coffee in cafes by the banks of the river. Dostoyevsky and Raskolnikov scurried feverishly through the downtown alleys on a mission—a gambling game, a meeting with God. King Lear and Othello played out their domestic madness in the local trailer park while Cordelia and Desdemona, in curlers and dungarees, pulled hidden bunks from the walls of tacky metal-clad trailers and slept in terror. And on the river, heading upstream into a lurid vermilion sunset scorched by forest fires, Marlowe's boat chugged toward Kurtz while Nick Adams fished along the banks.

As my knowledge of that imaginary world deepened I began to have trouble distinguishing between waking and dreaming, and between the literary figures of my imagination and those of the real streets around me. I spent most of my time somewhere in between, and it got me into car accidents, lost me jobs, and kept me on the wrong side of all the people who were trying to propagandize me into living in their world with them. It also made things difficult for those few generous souls who were attempting to teach me how to get around in my newly discovered world.

Except for what I could find in the public library, I had no substantive evidence that any world outside my immediate environment actually existed. I lived far away from that public library world, in a place where almost nothing was much more than a single generation older than I was. There were few old people, no old buildings, and the streets were just being paved and sidewalks being put in. My parents' generation was no help. They were the last generation of pioneers, and they were preoccupied with building personal fortunes, and along with it, the city they'd come to pioneer in. When they thought about anything beyond their immediate surroundings they looked only to the future, which they envisioned as one in which the walls of their houses would be papered with hundred-dollar bills. For them there was no past, and they made it no secret that they considered my interests a frivolous waste of time.

I had a singular ambition in life, one that for them was utterly incomprehensible: I wanted to be as great a poet as Shelley. How I arrived at so curious an ambition, I don't recall. My mother told me she read Shelley's poems to me when I was very young, and I knew the details of his life and untimely death in Italy from a romantic biography I'd found in the library. I was enthralled by him and by his life, even though I'd seen neither sailboat nor the sea, and understood next to nothing about the things he wrote of. I wrote horrible rhymed poetry myself, about what I decided were the Principles of Existence—Odes to Individualism, Elegies for Sincerity, Truth and Beauty. The poems were filled with the paraphernalia of 19th Century literature: larks, nightingales, Moorish castles, and desolations of every kind.

Yet something in the back of my mind told me I was doing it

wrong, and that I would have to leave my home town if I was ever to get it straight. So, as soon as I finished high school—I flunked, passing only English, history and day-dreaming in my final year—I saved a few hundred dollars and went off in search of that imaginary world where poetry was written, read, and listened to.

I had two or three subsidiary ambitions, none of which, naturally, I'd thought through very carefully. First of all, I wanted to live exactly as Shelley had. To do that, I knew, I would have to get as far away from home as I could possibly get. The other thing I wanted to do was to meet, in person, a Famous Writer, so I would know they really existed.

I did almost no planning. One of the advantages of being a poet who was one day going to be as great as Shelley was that I wasn't required to plan ahead like ordinary people. I hitch-hiked to Montreal, bought a one-way ticket on a rickety liner out of Montreal going to Southampton, and after six or seven days of wretched seasickness and a night train ride, I woke up in the YMCA in London, England, a few hundred feet from the British Museum.

I was fresh out of plans. I'd expected to walk out onto the street that first morning and be greeted by John Keats and Lord Byron.

"Ah, Shelley," Keats was to say, "Glad to have you back."

Byron was to announce that we were all leaving for Italy in the morning, and that Leigh Hunt and the Williamses were to accompany us on the voyage. I had only to pay my respects to Coleridge, Wordsworth, and William Blake before we departed.

But there was no one to greet me when I walked out onto Great Russell Street that first morning in London. The Great City was immense and gloomy and unfriendly, and I was 7000 miles from home and as frightened as I'd ever been in my life. I had about $200 in my pocket, and an edition of Shelley's poems in my knapsack. The waking dream I'd been living in now felt like a nightmare.

I walked across the street to the British Museum and sat down on the steps, wondering disconsolately what to do. It began to rain. I didn't have an umbrella, and I didn't think I could afford the price of admission to the museum, so I reached up and touched the claw of one of the stone lions to see if it might help. It didn't, and I trudged back to my room at the YMCA to do the first practical planning I'd ever done.

My mother had given me the address of an uncle, who had gone to England during the Second World War as a soldier and, falling in love with the island, had never come home. He lived on a farm somewhere in southern England, and was, according to my mother, married to a wonderfully elegant English Lady. When she gave me his address it had seemed unimportant. After all, I'd never met him, and I would soon be a Great Poet concerned only with the difficulties of composing great poems.

Now, however, that address seemed like the only valuable possession I had. I walked down to the reception desk and asked how to obtain my uncle's telephone number. The receptionist treated me in a kindly way, perhaps because she recognized that I was on the verge of tears. I explained to her, probably rather eloquently, what was wrong, and she was concerned enough with my plight that she found the number, dialed it, and even repeated my sad story to my uncle before she let me speak to him. I was grateful to her, and even more grateful when my uncle told me he'd be delighted to put me up for as long as I pleased, and provided explicit directions about how to reach him. My ambitions completely forgotten, I fled London within the hour.

I stayed with my uncle for almost three months. The farm was a pleasant place in the heart of the Sussex Downs. My uncle and my elegant English aunt were a kind of miracle. They were reasonably well-to-do—my uncle called himself a gentleman farmer—and they were the first real intellectuals I'd ever met. They took it upon themselves to smooth some of my rough edges, openly relishing the task even when my rough edges seemed to hide nothing but more rough edges. I came to trust them as I had not trusted any living human being, and gradually, and shyly, I told them why I had come to England.

My aunt laughed the gentlest of laughs, and hugged me.

"Well, young man," my uncle said gravely, "we can't make you as great a poet as Shelley, but we'll have to see what can be done about meeting your great writer."

He reeled off a list of famous writers who lived nearby or in London. I'd heard of none of them, but that didn't make the enumeration any less astonishing. He drew up a list of famous writers he thought I might like to meet, smiled at me, and left the room.

Several minutes later he returned with a tall stack of books.

"These are books by the writers on the list. Read through them, and we'll talk about which one you'd most like to meet."

I read the books at lightning speed. The writer I took for my first choice was John Osborne, the playwright. It was an easy choice. Osborne had recently been lionized for *Look Back in Anger* and the protagonist of the play resembled, in my mind at least, Shelley.

"Osborne lives near Hastings," my uncle told me. "If you're sure he's the one you'd like to meet, your aunt can drive you over that way in the morning."

Hastings was less than thirty miles from the farm. It took my aunt and me just over an hour to reach it, and by the time we arrived I was ill with anticipation.

"What should I say to him?" I asked her anxiously. "What if he doesn't want to speak to me?"

"Ask him a question," she said. "I'm sure you have a hundred of them. And of course he'll speak to you. Tell him who you are and how far you've come."

"I've only come thirty miles," I said, starting to panic.

"You've come all the way from Canada to see him," she laughed. "That should impress him."

My mind went blank when I tried to think of questions to ask John Osborne. All I could think of was to ask him if he liked Shelley.

My aunt got me to adjust the Shelley question. "Why don't you just ask Osborne if he's been influenced by the Romantic poets."

She made it sound so easy that I was relatively calm by the time we pulled up in front of Osborne's house. I'd been expecting something like Buckingham Palace, which I'd glimpsed on the way to Victoria station during my recent headlong retreat from London, and I was a little taken aback by the modest dimensions of his home. I sat in the car and stared at the door, frozen.

"Shouldn't you go and knock on the door now?" my aunt asked patiently.

I steeled myself, opened the door of the car, and got out. It closed behind me and I was alone, almost as alone as I'd felt that first day in London. John Osborne, a Famous Writer, wasn't going to speak to *me*. If he were going to, he would have opened the door by now and been walking down the sidewalk toward me with a smile on his luminous face. Instead, the door remained shut, the windows closed and shuttered.

As it happened, Osborne wasn't even in the country. He was, my aunt and I discovered a short time later, in the United States. I knocked on the door, knocked again, and even pounded on it in an ecstasy of relief when I realized no one was behind it. John Osborne was thousands of miles away. I walked back to the car.

"Would you like to see where the Battle of Hastings took place?" my aunt asked, thinking I needed to be consoled.

•

My second choice surprised my uncle. It was Cyril Connolly, the critic who wrote a book called *The Unquiet Grave* and had been the first British critic in the 1930s to recognize Henry Miller as an important new writer.

"Mr. Connolly lives in London," my uncle said, peering at me dubiously. "On St. James Park."

"Really? Do you know him personally?"

"I've never met the man," he said, offering no further explanation. "I thought you didn't like London."

"I was afraid of it," I admitted, "but maybe it's time I started to look around a little more."

The experience of *going* to meet John Osborne had altered my understanding of the structure of reality only slightly. I'd been in England for three months. I hadn't found any evidence of Shelley yet, nor of any other writer, except for John Osborne's house. Yet I was beginning to accumulate indisputable evidence that literature had a material existence. Osborne didn't really exist any more than Shelley did: not materially, and not in the present. But his house did, and its massive silence left me precisely where I preferred to be—in my imagination. Perhaps Connolly would oblige me in the same way, and in the same city where 150 years ago, Shelley himself had been.

My aunt drove me to Eastbourne, where I could catch the train to London. But before the station she took me to a little tobacconist's shop and bought me an expensive pipe and some Balkan Sobranie smoking tobacco. From there we went to a tea room. She ordered tea and sat me down.

"It's time for you to spread your wings now," she said. "You came to England to learn how to be as great a poet as Shelley, and it's time you got on with it."

I wanted to stay on the farm with them forever, but I didn't say so.

"Your uncle and I have given you a start here, and we both think you're ready," she went on when it became clear I didn't have anything to say. "You know you're always welcome, but if I were you I'd be careful not to stay too long again. The farm is a lovely place, but it's too easy. We're already part of the past, and you're part of the future."

"I don't want to live in the future," I said, after a moment's thought.

"The past can only teach you about the future," she said, smiling her gentlest smile. "You can't live in the past because it belongs to us. And you've got a train to catch."

•

I caught the train to London and my rendezvous with Cyril Connolly. As before, I stayed at the YMCA, spending the first evening staring at the ceiling and planning out what I would say to Connolly. I had his address, and a map of London that showed me how to get there. I was beginning to realize that I didn't have very much to say to my Famous Writer. All I really wanted from him was an acknowledgement that he existed apart from my imagination.

I arrived on Cyril Connolly's doorstep the next morning at precisely 11:00 in the morning. My uncle had prepared me with some care; 11:00 in the morning, he said, was the correct time to go calling on a stranger, and in my pocket were a number of calling cards he'd had printed up for me, each one with the street number of my parents' house, my town, my country, and my name at the top with the word "Esquire" after it.

I knocked on the door as politely as I could, and after a short wait a very fat man with a round face opened the door and looked me over carefully.

"Yes?"

"I'd like to speak with Mr. Connolly, please," I said, looking him in the eye as gravely as I could.

"May I say who it is that wishes to speak with him?" he asked imperiously.

I handed him one of my calling cards and told him my name. Happily, he didn't ask why I was calling on Mr. Connolly.

"One moment, I'll see if he is in."

This was it. I stifled an impulse to run away: any second, Cyril Connolly, an actual Famous Writer, would be standing in front of me asking me to explain my presence in his world.

But instead, the fat man reappeared.

"I'm afraid Mr. Connolly is indisposed," he told me in an apologetic tone. "He won't be available for some time, unfortunately, as he is working. Perhaps if you called back at some later date?"

I nearly fainted with relief, but I managed to thank the fat man for his time—I assumed he was Connolly's butler—and asked him to pass on my regards to the Great Man. My uncle had coached me on this one, and I said it with such sincerity the rotund butler threw me a crumb.

"I'll inform Mr. Connolly that you stopped by, and I'm sure he'll regret not having had the opportunity to speak with you."

I thanked him with great warmth and dashed off down the street in an ecstasy of relief.

I wandered through the streets of London in that condition for several hours before it dawned on me that I was again fresh out of plans, and that once more I was thousands of miles from home, without friends in a strange and ancient city. I'd failed for the second time to secure evidence that famous writers truly existed, although I'd come much closer on this attempt.

On an impulse, I returned to the YMCA and walked over to the British Museum. My uncle had mentioned that many great books had been written in the reading room of the British Museum and while the chances of seeing a famous writer there weren't good, there should at least be writers of some sort there. The museum, he told me, was free, so it could serve any number of purposes, including providing refuge from the rain.

There weren't any writers—famous or otherwise—in the reading room. Everybody was reading, and a few people were turning the pages on books and jotting things down. I drifted through and walked over to several large glass cases containing books.

The sign above one of them read SHELLEY MANUSCRIPTS. I froze. Inside the case were a number of booklets, on which words had been written in red ink. The handwriting was a scrawl, curiously childish, and almost illegible. I got down on my knees to obtain a better view, my heart pounding.

I was staring at Shelley's poems, the same ones that were in my edition of the Complete Works, and I was discovering, in that fading red ink, the most profound and indelible lesson life had thus far offered me. As I kneeled in front of that magical case and gazed at the manuscripts, my hands pressed reverently against the glass, my understanding of reality cracked, broke apart into a million pieces, rearranged itself, and became whole again. I imagined Shelley's hand and arm, writing each word, one after another, across the page, just as, in my fumbling way, I did when I wrote. Here and there in the manuscript words had been crossed out, lines rearranged, whole verses deleted. On one of the pages was a blotch of ink—perhaps someone had entered the room and playfully pushed his arm. Was it a food-stain I saw on another page? There was no denying the shocking truth before me. Shelley, the great poet Shelley, had struggled to write each line. He had played with people, talked, eaten food; just like a real person.

•

I spent nearly a week in the museum, adjusting to my revised sense of reality. Again and again I returned to gaze at the red ink of the Shelley manuscripts, soaking up their astonishing truth.

As the new reality settled, I examined what it had done to my world. The ground was more stable now, and the objects I could see assumed an oddly human scale. And I had a job. To be as great a poet as Shelley, I would have to work at it, write every single one of my great poems down. Shelley wasn't going to help me. He'd been dead for nearly a century and a half. Meeting a famous writer wouldn't help either, since famous writers were just people who worked hard.

I didn't know at the time that I had in fact already met with and spoken to a famous writer. It wasn't until I saw a photograph of Cyril Connolly years later that I understood who his butler had been.

I had a little time left in England before my money ran out and I would have to go home. I checked out of the YMCA and rented a small room near King's Cross Station, a room that had a desk and a reading lamp in it. I got out my edition of Shelley from my knapsack and put it on the desk. Then I put it back again, took out a notebook and a pen, and began to make another kind of world.

On the Dangers of Watching Gangster Movies

I had a girlfriend once who had a peculiar talent for never laughing at anything at the right time. When people told her jokes, she would laugh midway through, usually at some turn of phrase that tugged at the cross-circuited part of her sense of humour, and more often than not she would stare at the joke-teller in stony silence when the punchline came. I never told her jokes.

Once I fell down a set of stairs while in her company. This wasn't a terribly unusual occurrence for me, since I'm clumsy. It's a characteristic I prefer to think of as similar to absent-mindedness, sort of like 'absent-bodiedness.'

Whatever caused it, I fell down those stairs and hurt myself, badly twisting an ankle. I rolled over on my back, squealing loudly, expecting her to hurry down after me, ready with endearments and a patch-kit. Instead, she was leaning against the wall at the top of the stairwell, helpless with laughter. Instantly I wished that she'd be so taken over by her laughter that she'd fall down the stairs after me, but that wasn't to be. This is not a wholly just universe, and I slithered around in the filthy street for several minutes clutching my ankle and whimpering in agony before she was able to stumble down the stairs, still giggling, to ask the usual rhetorical question asked of people in extremity: "Are you hurt? Are you going to be okay?"; followed by the circumstantially tricky question: "What should I do?"

It was the end of our relationship. I accused her of being sadistic and reptilian about my misfortune, and refused to forgive her. It's too bad. She was very good looking, and if I'd been paying attention to what she was seeing instead of insisting on my self-concerned moral causalities, I might have learned what it was she found so funny. But this isn't the story I'm here to tell. It's just that I know she's going to be helpless with laughter and when she reads this. Maybe she'll be standing near some stairs.

•

Okay. So let's get to it. My story concerns Good and Evil, an ancient brawl that usually doesn't offer much of interest to jokers like my old girlfriend. Now that we've officially defeated Fascism, Monarchism and most of the other Large Evils in the world; and now that we wake up in the middle of the night wondering if maybe *we're* the Evil, the only figures of evil we can all agree on are gangsters.

Did you ever notice that in those old movies about gangsters there are never any accidents? None of them ever falls down stairs, for instance. Their evil is always malevolent and competent, and that is *why* it is fearful. That their evil is always defeated is a tribute to the power of Good. The gangsters are defeated by the sheer number of bodies Good throws in their path. They are crushed beneath the mass of the well-intentioned blunderers who have God or Business or Elliot Ness on their side. I can already hear my ex-girlfriend starting to break up with laughter.

•

Robert Billings and Stanley Brooks were small-time punks in Akron, Ohio. As you can tell from their names, neither was Sicilian, a malfunction in the order of things that both men resented deeply. Most of their adult lives had been spent either in jail or in bungling crimes that would soon put them back in jail. This is not to imply that they were amusing. They weren't. They were not nice people, not even if one stretches one's liberal sympathies for the culturally disadvantaged. One of their specialties was breaking bones in people's faces. And Billings, in particular, enjoyed pulling his victim's eyeballs out of their heads, a predilection that earned him a modest reputation for cruelty among his own professional colleagues. Billings and Brooks plied their trade for money when they could, but if no one would pay them, they'd do it just for the sheer joy of crunching a square john.

You can therefore imagine how pleased they were when an Akron car dealer approached them to ask if they would make a hit on a certain rival. It was their first hit, and it meant, in their eyes anyway, a move in the direction of the Big Time, and the possibility of careers in the upper echelons of organized crime, maybe even in New York or California. Big cars. High-powered rifles. Black gloves and swift exits to airports.

Each man owned a hand-gun. Billings had an army-issue .45, and he referred to it affectionately as "The Cannon". Brooks possessed a .357 magnum, a weapon legendary for its high muzzle velocity and destructive effect on blocks of wood and other offending items. The slugs it used were smaller than those from a .45 but they travelled at a significantly higher speed, exploding on contact with any solid object. The .45 tended to make tunnels; the .357 made a smaller entrance, but on the back side, it built a parking lot. I hope you're interested in this sort of detail.

Despite their big-time ambitions, the plan Billings and Brooks made to carry out the contract involved no rifles, no black gloves, and no airports. On the contrary, their plan was stunningly simple. They intended to pick up their target outside a bar, beat him senseless, shoot him to death, and then throw his weighted body into the Cuyahoga river. If the plan had any twist to it, it was in this last part. You remember the Cuyahoga River. It's the one that is so infamously polluted that it combusted spontaneously outside Cleveland a few years ago. It took the Cleveland Fire Department several days to put out the blaze. Billings and Brooks, in their way, meant to utilize this bit of local natural history, believing that the river would dissolve the corpse in a matter of days.

Their first difficulty was a lifestyle difficulty. Their intended victim was neither a car dealer like their employer, nor was he a gangster. In fact, he was a school teacher. He didn't hang around in bars; he didn't even drink. When they pointed this out to their employer, wondering out loud what he had against a school teacher, the car dealer intimated that something prurient was involved.

"The bastard is screwing my wife," he said, "and I want him wasted before it goes any further."

"How about your old lady," Billings asked. "You want us to blow her away too?"

"If we can catch them together we'll give you two for the price of one," Brooks added, thinking to appeal to his employer's business acumen.

"Just the guy," said the car dealer. "Don't go getting creative on me."

Robbed of a scenario they were comfortable with, our protagonists picked up their victim in front of his school. They picked him up with at least fifty cheering students for an audience, most of whom thought it was terrifically funny, because the victim was the school's drama teacher, and had a reputation for innovative teaching methods. Some of the students who saw the abduction assumed that their teacher was being made the victim of some sort of practical joke, and still others supposed he was demonstrating some principle relating to drama.

The school teacher himself thought it was a practical joke, and for several blocks offered no resistance. He was waiting to see what hilarity would develop, and on the whole, wished the entire venture the very best. Billings and Brooks had him between them, in the front seat of Billings' aging Buick, and it was only when Brooks broke the teacher's nose with a well-placed elbow that the teacher began to realize that he was in some sort of real trouble. He was not without courage, and without a word, attempted to duplicate the gesture on Billings, who was driving the car. When he succeeded, the car made an elegant and symmetrical detour across the front lawns of a dozen Akron homes before Billings recovered his senses and brought the automobile to a stop in the middle of a modest rose garden.

Both villains drew their guns and pistol-whipped their victim into unconsciousness, this time to an audience of home owners, who, cautious folk that they were, did not interfere. They merely formed a ring around the Buick and watched the proceedings as if it were a television program, wondering why Billings and Brooks didn't look more like Starsky and Hutch. At length Brooks noticed them, rolled down the window and brandished the .357 magnum. They scattered.

"We better roll out of here," he suggested to his partner, who, with better concentration on the task at hand, had noticed nothing amiss.

"Why?" he asked.

"There's some johns. They might get the licence number."

"Oh yeah. Okay. This turkey's out of it anyway."

Billings re-started the car, ran it across a rosebed, through the low border fence, and bumped back onto the street.

"What now?" he asked Brooks.

"We take him to the river. Then we knock him off and ditch the sack."

"The what?"

"The sack, stupid. The body."

"Oh yeah. Right."

So they drove cheerfully to the Cuyahoga River, oblivious to their bleeding victim, who, in quite a different way, was oblivious to them. Billings was whistling a Stevie Nicks tune, the words to which he could never quite get the sense of.

As they approached the river, however, the teacher came to and began to struggle wildly.

"Pull over," Brooks yelled, holding the thrashing man by the throat. "We'll blow him away right here!"

And that's just was they did. Billings pushed his .357 Magnum against the man's left side and fired. Brooks, with his gun in his left hand, and still holding the school teacher by the throat with his right arm, dug his .45 into the back of his ribs and fired at the same instant.

Both bullets passed through the victim's body without coming into contact with bone nor, miraculously, with a vital organ. Billings' bullet lodged itself in Brooks' spine, literally blowing it to smithereens. Brooks' bullet found Billings heart. Both of them died within a split second of each other.

A troop of firemen who were inspecting the river happened to be passing by, and they heard the shots. The school teacher survived, although he was in critical condition for a number of days. Later on he gave the hospital staff some trouble because he suffered from paroxysms of uncontrollable laughter, and burst his stitches several times.

The car dealer was punished by law in an appropriate manner. The school teacher and the car dealer's ex-wife now live on a quiet street in Akron, secure within, if somewhat chastened by, the power of love. I don't know where my ex-girlfriend is.

You Have to Be Somewhere Tonight

Inside a gas station northeast of Edmonton, Alberta, on a chilly evening in late April, six young men wearing dark green padded coats and peaked caps of the same colour pour oily coffee into styrofoam cups and stir in lumps of white sugar and whitener. Then, smiling the broad smiles of men exercising a proud and precious right, they drink it. They talk to one another more loudly than they need to, and they bump each other boisterously, spilling nearly as much coffee as they drink. Who are they?

I first see these young men as I walk into the gas station's office to pay for the gas I've pumped into the tank of my car.

The young men glance over at me without much curiosity as I enter, and then go on talking; drinking their coffee as if I do not exist. I find the young men much more interesting than they find me. They are dressed alike, and they are dressed quite peculiarly. Since they're all about the same age, I wonder if they are perhaps in some unfamiliar branch of the Armed Forces. This is, after all, northern Alberta, where the government uses the chill and empty countryside to field-test everything from missiles to chemical weapons, for itself and for any government with which it is friendly.

But after a slightly more careful examination, I'm pretty well certain that the young men are not from the military: several wear thick spectacles and they are ill-groomed and undisciplined. Yet there is a unanimity about them, and they're enjoying themselves the way people do when they believe in some powerful authority that provides them with all they need to know about one another and the world around them.

I pay for my gas, and on the way back out to my car I ask the pump jockey about the young men, wondering aloud if they have anything to do with the military.

"Hutterites," the pump jockey laughs. "Hutterite hoodlums. Fresh out of God's army. They wouldn't hurt a fly."

I'm in no hurry, and I start my car and sit awhile, watching them. I've heard something of the Hutterites. They're an ascetic Christian sect that has prospered in the cold climate of the Canadian prairies by practising economic self-sufficiency and a strict social orthodoxy.

I'd prefer to think of Hutterites as tall men in baggy black suits, heavy beards and wide-brimmed hats, not as scratchy-faced punks in padded green coats. But as I think it through, I realize I'm remembering Hutterites as I saw them in a small agricultural town near the American border years ago. And as the two images mesh, I recall something else: a recent newspaper story about the government being petitioned to stop land sales to the sect because their neighbours felt the Hutterites were becoming too powerful and too well-organized for ordinary farmers to compete with.

These young men, then, might be a kind of commando group, out to terrorize isolated, independent, individualistic, alienated citizens into selling their property at half its value. If I were more paranoid, I might talk myself into thinking that this small town was being brutalized by these hoodlums and others like them, and that, in self-defense, the citizens encourage them to prey on passing strangers. If this were a big American city, such a thing could easily occur. But here? A thought as silly as the hoodlums themselves.

Dusk is falling, and the night promises to be a cold one. I reach over and turn on the car's heater. The warmth pours across my shoes and I ease into the creature comfort, feeling secure in my humming environment—a small piece of the city.

The Hutterites are still bouncing around inside the gas station, still pushing and shoving, squinting through their filthy glasses at one another and at the world. All they want is to be like those carefree kids they've seen on television and in magazines, and in fact they are, in a clumsy sort of way. Their rough macho maleness, long submerged beneath the religious severity of their sect, has burst out like a swarm of hornets, and buzzes in the cold air. The more I look at them the more they resemble my world, and a thought cuts through me like a gust of wind.

Maybe, out in the cold hills, the dour, industrious Hutterites have all become like us, crouched around colour television sets, picking and choosing what they want of civilization from the satellite dish on the roof. Maybe they too have given up the obscure struggle to make a new world, and are selecting their reality from the rainbow media stew: junksports from Florida; blue movies from Los Angeles; reruns of Jack Webb police operas from Akron, Ohio; heavy metal rock videos from New York. I feel their blue eyes clouding as they are seduced and transformed by the bewildering transference of electronic energy—secular now, spectators in the sterile homogenization of human reality.

Maybe these hoodlums are the first visible signals, the first sloppy raindrops in the storm that will finally leave us with one world, one common fate. For now, all we can see is what the hoodlums see—a cornucopia of consumer packages: individually wrapped chemical cheese slices, deodorants, hypoallergenic creams, Oreos, Diet Coke, Hostess Twinkies, high octane gasoline and beer, all carefully designed to relieve us of the necessity for discriminatory perception. The storm will leave that one world crouching passively in front of colour television screens, waiting for the next miraculous commodity, the next denatured thrill, the next sterilized third world catastrophe or overthrown government.

•

Inside the gas station the Hutterite hormones reach a frenzied peak. The hoodlums are near riot. And in answering celebration, above us in the sky, the cloud has rolled back for the onslaught of moonlight and hoar-frost. The moon is full. We can do whatever we want, have whatever we choose, the Hutterite hoodlums and I; provided we stay on or near the highway. We are languishing in the laps of luxuries none of us can quite seem to experience. We can have whatever we choose, but the choices are pointless.

I look out behind me in the rear-view mirror. A row of neon signs: Gulf, McDonalds, Esso, Kentucky Fried Chicken. The signs, each familiar, trail off into mere coloured light. This asphalt strip, like ten thousand others like it, is the true measure of our wealth. Of all the things our wealth and liberty could have made, this is all there is: asphalt, franchised consumer opportunities useful only for profit-taking and the gathering of capital, human beings telling lies to one another to mark out the territorial rituals of competitive brotherhood, stuffing their bodies with chemicals while the full moon rides by unadorned by even sentimental attention.

Capital entertains, addicts, turns every liberty to social violence or to privacy. Even here. I've been driving since dawn, and each and every particularity of the natural landscape has been matched and overwhelmed by human constructions that are significant only for their absolute lack of particularity. They could be found and are found anywhere on the continent. And after twelve hours of it, no conclusions are necessary, no villains appear on the horizon wearing black. Who could have planned this, or predicted it? No one. It is crazier than the wildest of science fictions.

Maybe those grim old Hutterites of the past were right. They were at least correct in their belief that almost everything is more important than self-gratification. And they fought this world, and for a time at least, they were successful. For all their intellectual rigidity and their distaste for physical reality they have honored its materials better than the rest of us have.

And now they have been defeated. Their children stand around inside a gas station loading their bodies with chemicals while their elders make plans to buy up the planet, just like Florida real estate moguls.

They will be more like us than we are, these newcomers. They will be more aggressive, more energetic, less constrained by experience. They are the embodied second thoughts that come from watching one's loved ones starve in the midst of abundance. And soon, these people will be more violent than we are, we who have grown weary of thrills.

The hoodlums begin to break up their party, crumpling the styrofoam cups and tossing them into a garbage can made from a forty-five gallon oil drum. One of them places his cup upside down on the floor and stamps on it, startling his comrades into more laughter. They push open the door, straggle out to a yellow Chevrolet travel-all and crowd inside it, slamming the doors shut, one after another. The one who's driving starts the motor, letting it roar for a moment before he slams the shift-lever of the automatic transmission into reverse, and the truck fishtails backward through the parking lot, bucking and thumping in and out of the potholes. Then all four headlights go on, and off go the Hutterites into the northern darkness, looking for trouble, thinking they can avoid the adventure and dull difficulty our now-common destiny has waiting for them.

I light a cigarette, roll down the car window and send a stream of smoke out into the chilly air, just like a private detective. I catch sight of the full moon, even here stained with industrial filth. Down the road in the distance are the yellow arches of a McDonald's. I still have another hundred miles to go and I'll drive it with the same threat hanging over my head that hangs over the heads of the Hutterite hoodlums inside their travel-all—everyone has to be somewhere tonight.

The Revolutionary

If this were a novel, and if I were Fyodor Dostoyevsky, this would be an easy story to tell. It would probably be a very long novel, too, filled with casual conversation and odd characters running around at their wits' ends. But this is decidedly and deliberately just a story, and Mr. Dostoyevsky has been dead for a century. The circumstances leave me with a very troubling problem. You see, I knew an important character from one of Dostoyevsky's novels. For a while, he was my best friend.

The Dostoyevsky character will remain un-named, in order, as they say, to protect the innocent, and (a far-off possibility) to interest some future student of comparative literature. This is therefore a detective story and your job as the detective is to detect the hidden origins of the events I will relate, and at the same time to predict their outcome.

Let me stir the brew right at the outset by admitting that for several weeks I too was a character from one of Dostoyevsky's novels. It began while I was in Paris trying, in my romantic way, to decide whether or not I wished to continue living. I was eighteen years old, and life seemed both terribly beautiful and terribly unjust. Like a character from the Dostoyevsky novel I was reading at the time, I felt compelled to express first of all my independence from the injustice of the world, and secondly my worship of its beauty, by committing the ultimate act of independence and self-renunciation: killing myself on behalf of a righteous cause.

Luckily for me I couldn't find a suitably righteous cause—I spoke so little French I was unable to discuss the weather, let alone offer my existential proposition to anyone. So instead I got on a boat back to North America, where I've since learned how difficult it is to accurately worship beauty and denounce injustice. I suppose that the character I became during those few weeks is still lurking somewhere in my personality, but this story isn't about my personality, and you can end that area of speculation.

I met Peter at university. I was several years older than he was, and I was newly married. On the first day of classes, I saw him in the row ahead of me watching the professor give his lecture. He was tall, blonde and very thin, and he wore wire-rimmed glasses very much like my own. That's probably why I noticed him initially. During the lecture, though, I noticed that Peter kept whispering the word 'beautiful' about every thirty seconds no matter what was being said. I figured him right away for a wacko, and I was, therefore, interested.

In those days a lot of students spent most of the time in states of altered consciousness—we believed that altering our consciousnesses was the true subject of education—so Peter didn't seem unusual or perturbing. After all, it was 1967, and LSD had recently come into wide and extremely impure distribution. Those of us who weren't trying to maladjust our DNA chains with it were smoking any herb that resembled marijuana. The dope-dealers were cleaning the supermarkets out of parsley, sage, rosemary and thyme, and Peace and Love were just beginning their lurid descent into corporate profitability. My entire generation was looking for any alternative to the conventional wisdom of the Cold War, and nearly everywhere we looked we were finding those alternatives.

Peter was looking harder than most. I think he came from one of those nameless ennui-soaked suburbs of Los Angeles, and no matter how he tried to lose it, he reeked of it. I don't know what drew him to me. Maybe it was because my brand of ennui served no location or identity other than my own. But whatever it was, he introduced himself a few days after that first class, named a mutual acquaintance, and said he'd overheard me saying, as he put it, "a few things I go for."

"You're an American, aren't you," I asked coldly. "What do you want?"

I made a virtue of being hostile to strangers. Since, in my mind, I was the most interesting person I knew, I considered my time valuable, and I suspected everybody of trying to waste it.

"I'm dodging the draft," Peter answered in a mild voice.

Now, being a draft dodger, in 1967, meant an automatic ticket to everything. No one asked questions of you, and you were accorded the instant status of one who is courageous, intelligent and aware, because if you weren't all of those things, you'd be slogging through the jungles of Vietnam trying to kill people. Despite my feelings about my own perfectness, I was able to recognize real status when I saw it, and I deferred to it: I apologized profusely to Peter for my rudeness.

We soon discovered that we had some things in common—not surprising, since we were both literature students and were taking many of the same courses. Peter questioned me about the sorts of things I was interested in, which was quite a long list and included an accompanying tirade against all the things I wasn't interested in. To every off-the-wall opinion I threw across the table at him, he responded with the same 'beautiful!' refrain I'd heard at that first lecture. It sounded better than it had before, and I swiftly drew him into my small social circle—my wife and the few others who were willing to put up with me.

It was weeks before I heard much of anything other than 'beautiful' from Peter, and more weeks before I became curious about what he might actually think about the world around me. I didn't know it, but by that time it was too late: he had only a past, and his opinions were indistinguishable from my own.

I didn't notice. But since the only ideas I was interested in were my own, my only outlet for being curious about other people lay in the area of appearances, and Peter's appearance, the more I looked at him, was extremely curious.

He had an awkward tilt to his head, which at first I thought was his way of listening carefully. But then I realized he spoke, walked, and even ran with his head held in the same insect-like posture. I questioned him about it, and he explained that he'd fallen from a tree on Mount Tamalpais near San Francisco. He'd been flipped on LSD and was trying to touch Heaven. Instead, he said, a branch of the World Tree had snapped under his weight and he'd broken his neck. Peter related this without any apparent sense of irony. If he hadn't fallen, his attitude implied, he might now be in Heaven.

I'd been given an important clue, but its significance was lost on me. His actions struck me as foolish and elegant at the same time, and I couldn't decide if he was a fallen angel or a praying mantis. It was quite all right with me if he was both, just so long as he didn't impose either identity on me.

Peter attached himself to my wife, who was more accommodating than I was, and talked less. Their friendship seemed natural enough to me; they were the same age and shared a day-to-day preoccupation with drugs and organic food that I didn't have any inclination for.

When he moved into a student commune adjoining the house my wife and I lived in, and then more or less moved in with us, I was pleased that we had the company. The three of us drove to classes together, discussed the books we were reading together (or rather, while they listened, I discussed the books all of us were reading) and more often than not, we ate our meals together.

It was Peter who introduced me to the Revolution, which, in my self-absorption, I hadn't really noticed. Because it was outside my usual self-occupied orbit, I demanded that he define it in very specific terms.

"It ain't that easy, man," Peter said, slipping into an odd drawl. "Revolutions are invisible. By the time they become visible they're all over. It's all around you. I mean, the Revolution is everywhere."

"Yeah, yeah. Is the revolution drugs?" I referred to it in lower case; he used upper case.

"That's part of it, man, that's part of it. Drugs teach you to see in a different way, without the doors of perception cluttered up with everyday logic."

"What about war? Is stopping war part of it?"

"Oh, yeah man. Beautiful. Wow." The drawl was heavier now.

"Stopping the War is what it's all about. I mean, the War is a symbol for everything we have to change about this country."

"This country isn't at war," I pointed out, my eyes narrowing. "Only the United States is."

"Yeah, well, the Revolution is happening everywhere. You know. War-schmore. The war belongs to everyone."

"What about sex? Is the revolution got to do with sex?"

It was Peter's turn to squint.

"Oh yeah, right," he said. "For sure. Sex has got to be made easier to get than it is now. We've got to stop thinking of our bodies as property, because when we do, sex will turn into a groovy kind of freedom, like, into sharing."

That happened to coincide with my own foggy ideas. I wanted sex to be more free, and I wanted to share my body with quite a lot of the women I was meeting, but I was uneasy about where the boundaries of the new freedom were supposed to be. I had a vague list of things I wanted to see and experience sexually, vague but nonetheless exhaustive. I had some doubts that I would ever get to experience what I wanted, because I was married and that meant monogamy. I loved my wife, and it tormented me that my vague and exhaustive list seemed to contradict the tenderness and raw need I felt for her.

•

Between our house and Peter's commune was a vacant lot. It was part of the commune property, and surrounding it was an overgrown cedar hedge. At one time it had been a closed garden of some elegance. A small creek ran along one side of it and our dining room looked out over it. Several years before we moved into the house the commune had made an unsuccessful attempt to grow vegetables there, ripping out a sizeable portion of the old planting. The area they'd cultivated was now flat and grassy and the rest was a tangled ruin of shrubs and neglected perennials. The vacant lot disturbed me. Peter and the rest of the commune called it "the garden". At every opportunity I carefully called it "the vacant lot", referring pointedly to the commune's lack of agrarian interest. They were guilty, in my opinion, of moral diseconomy. Worse, the vacant lot was disorder of a brand new variety. If the Revolution was going to rebuild the world, it seemed to me that it had better pay closer attention to its material base than did the decaying regime it was planning to replace.

I even re-dug a section of the commune's garden and planted vegetables of my own, but the seedlings had barely broken the surface of the soil before the commune members played a drug-induced midnight touch football game and trampled every one of them.

After that I stared out into the ruin each evening at dinner, wondering what to do with it. I stayed disturbed until Peter, uncharacteristically, became irritable.

"Why do you keep staring at the garden?" he said.

"It's a vacant lot," I replied, primly. "A garden has to be taken care of."

"Then take care of it," he sneered. "Don't just stare at it."

"You bastards will just trample everything I try."

"Then do something so dramatic it can't be trampled," he said, more thoughtfully. "Get their attention that way."

I stewed for several days before it came to me. I would take Peter's suggestion literally: I'd turn the vacant lot into a theatre.

"What play do we put on?" Peter asked when I told him.

"I dunno. Shakespeare, I guess," I said, after a second's thought. "How about *King Lear*?"

"You just want to be King Lear," my wife objected. That was only partially true, and I argued strenuously that my real reason for wanting to put it on was that casting it would be so much fun.

"How about Lucille Ball and Phyllis Diller as Goneril and Regan?" I said.

"Aw, far out!" Peter said, and then talked me out of it by pointing out that the play was too long, and for amateurs, which even I was willing to agree we were, too slow.

"How about *A Midsummer Night's Dream*?" I suggested.

Peter thought for a moment.

"Everyone does that play," he said, knowing I wouldn't want to do something everybody did. "How about *A Winter's Tale*?"

I didn't know the play, but I wasn't about to admit it. "What do you think?" I asked my wife, democratically.

She was genuinely startled. Then a troubled expression crossed her face, and she stared at Peter for a moment before she spoke.

"It's a wonderful play," she said.

"Okay, then," Peter said. "That's the one."

I'd missed another clue.

•

Peter and I began the task of casting the play and planning the sets. I appointed myself both the star and director, but since I still had to read the play, I left the casting entirely to Peter and my wife, assigning to myself the task of building the sets. The garden, with it surrounding foliage and barren trampled centre, suddenly seemed almost perfect. There didn't appear to be much to do.

I was wrong.

"The one thing we have to get," Peter advised, "is the statue of Hermione."

"Right," I agreed blankly. "The statue of Hermione."

There were some cedar poles lying around in the commune's yard. Someone had fixated, very temporarily, on carving totem poles, and after obtaining a number of fine-grained fifteen-foot cedar poles and mutilating several of them without obtaining the slightest resemblance to a totem pole, they had abandoned the project. Peter suggested that we put one of them up and use that for a statue, proposing that I could paint the figure of a woman on it.

"Localism," he said, "is what we're supposed to be learning, right? So it's fitting that our statue of Hermione should be a mixture of Shakespeare and aboriginal art."

His enthusiasm was both convenient and slightly contagious. I chose one of the poles, and spent the next several evenings digging holes and dragging and pulling the heavy pole into position, while Peter and my wife sat in the house phoning prospective actors, rereading the play, and smoking dope. Occasionally they'd venture out into the garden, giggle themselves into exhaustion at my efforts, and disappear back into the house. They left the statue up to me, almost as if by design. I decided that Peter disliked lifting heavy weights, and found ways to do it on my own.

It took me four nights to complete the statue. By the third night, after stringing a set of lights in the garden and working until past midnight, I had the pole erect, and had drawn an exaggerated outline of a woman on it.

The pole was half obscured by the branches of the surrounding trees, which seemed both appropriate and fortuitous to me—I was no artist, and the foliage would serve localism and obscure my lousy craftsmanship. I stood and admired Hermione for a few minutes, then called out to Peter and my wife to come out and praise me.

Nothing. They weren't in the house. I looked across the garden but could see no lights in the commune. I assumed that they'd gone for a walk, something they'd taken to doing lately. There was a joint on the kitchen table; I was tired, and after I smoked the joint I was really tired, so I went to bed.

They were in the kitchen having breakfast when I breezed downstairs the next morning.

"Up and at 'em early, I see," I said, feeling cheerful at the thought of my now-erect statue standing in the garden. "Listen, I've got to go downtown and get the paint so I can finish Hermione. I take it you guys can do without me this morning. Then I've got to go up to the university this afternoon."

"Okay," my wife said, matching my cheerfulness.

Peter was less obliging.

"Actually, I wish you'd stay around this morning," he said. "I'd like to go over some of the parts with you so we can get them right."

I had to weasel out of that rather carefully. The reason I had to go up to the university was to read the play. I'd been so involved in putting up the pole that I still hadn't looked at the text. There were only a few days left before midsummer's night, the date we'd chosen for the production's grand opening, run and final performance.

"Maybe tonight," I said evasively. "You two don't need me until then."

"Nope, I guess we don't," said my wife with her earlier cheerfulness, and with enough finality that Peter didn't argue.

It was hard to get Peter to argue. It was probably the only thing about him I didn't like, since arguing was both my favorite pastime and my chief study-tool. Trying to argue with Peter was like trying to nail jello to a wall. I would contradict some leading statement he made, and four sentences further on find him standing precisely on the argumentative ground I had set up to defend. If I shifted my ground, and *attacked* my original position—something that was often difficult for me to locate—he would pull his intellectual disappearing act and pop up in my *new* position.

So naturally, that night I was taken aback when he came out to watch me painting the statue and started an argument.

"Why don't you stop being such an asshole?" he said.

"Since when does painting a statue make me an asshole?" I replied, nonplussed. "I know it isn't very good. But I notice that no one else has offered to do it."

"We were busy," he said aggressively. "That isn't it anyway. It's awful, but that isn't it. You're just being an asshole lately."

Peter had hit my Achilles' heel. I was willing to attack anyone, but I feared being attacked. One of the mysteries in my life, perhaps the most perplexing one for me, was that nobody seemed to notice that I was a phoney. In over my head. Stupid.

I beat a retreat.

"You wanted to talk to me about the play," I said meekly. "So talk about that."

"Do you know what this play is about?" he said accusingly, in the same aggressive tone.

"Sure," I said. (I'd read the last half of the play that afternoon.) "It's about forgiveness."

"It's about jealousy," he contradicted. "And infidelity."

"That's your opinion," I retorted, discharging my best weapon immediately.

"Don't you see it?" he asked, almost incredulously. "Don't you agree?"

I shrugged. I knew the play was about forgiveness, but I wasn't exactly sure what it was the characters in the play were forgiving one another for. I'd read the play thinking about the statue, and that was about all I knew from my reading—that a statue had come to life, and that everything came out right in the end.

"I don't understand everything, you know," I mumbled defensively. "Some things make sense, and others don't."

Peter seemed defeated. I couldn't tell if it was by my humility or my stupidity. I was still on the chair I'd been standing on to paint the statue. I got down, and on an impulse, pulled a leaf from an overhanging tree. The leaf wa yellow, with only a little green at its heart, as if it had been blowing in the wind too long. I handed it to Peter.

"Have you ever looked at a leaf? A simple leaf from a tree?"

"What's that?" he said, looking at me suspiciously. "An allegory?"

"Nope, I'm not talking about an allegory. It's a leaf, only a leaf."

"So?"

"So the leaf is good. I understand *that* much. If we all concentrate on it, everything will be okay. The mother-in-laws will die, and the children will live."

Peter was staring at me with his mouth open. Something in the way he'd attacked me earlier was forcing me to carry out the benediction I was offering him.

"I don't know what you're talking about," he said, shrinking away from me. He dropped the leaf and I reached down to pick it up. I tried to hand it to him but he skittered away through the trees like an apparition.

Feeling better, I turned back to the statue. I put a few finishing touches on it, went into the house, smoked some dope and fell asleep on the couch.

•

Peter was over for breakfast the next morning, apologetic.

"Never mind," I said, grandly, "it was just your dope and my Gnosticism."

We were studying the Gnostics in one of the courses we were taking together. My view of Gnosticism was fairly confused; not surprising since I was reading the dense texts paragraph by paragraph, and so far I'd gotten through only about five pages. I'd put together my juvenile knowledge of Agnosticism with what I knew from reading Russian novels and come up with Gnosticism. I wasn't getting much contradiction of this from my continued research, since a single paragraph on the Gnostics seemed to put me to sleep.

"What do you think about the Gnostics?" he asked, unexpectedly humble.

"They're okay," I shrugged. "As far as I understand them."

"Well," Peter said, almost to no one, "I'm glad we know they're significant."

"Why?"

"Because if I wasn't sure they were significant, I'd sure wonder why I was believing in them."

"Nobody asked you to believe in them," I pointed out. "You're supposed to understand things, not believe in them."

Peter looked up from the toast he was coating with raspberry jam and stared at me for a minute before he went on.

"I like believing in things. If you can't believe in what you're doing, there's no point in doing anything."

"Maybe there is no point in doing anything. You're acting like you believe in God. Maybe there's nothing worth believing. That doesn't change the way the world really is. It just means that understanding things is the only thing that's automatically worth working at."

"Why?" Peter said, genuine confusion in his expression.

"Because if it's all bullshit and illusion, and we're all alone in an indifferent universe, then each of us has to make order for ourselves. You can do it with police or transcendental meditation or whatever you like. But the only thing that can't be taken away from you is your understanding."

"You're nuts," he said, glancing across the table at my wife as he said it, for confirmation. She was staring out the window. She'd heard it before.

"Okay," I said. "Who cares?"

"She does," Peter screeched, pointing at my wife. "And so do I!"

He got up from the table without finishing his toast and rushed out the door like a swarm of bees was chasing him.

"What's got into him?" I asked my wife. She merely raised her eyebrows and went on with her breakfast without answering.

•

Peter didn't show up all day, and after dinner I walked through the garden to the commune to find out what was wrong with him. I was worried about the play—there was a lot that needed to be done—and I was beginning, already, to miss his company. On the way through the garden I glanced up at the statue. Someone had pinned a Playboy fold-out over my representation of a woman. I gazed at it for a moment, at the miniaturized yet oversized torso, the empty but sweet face, the impossibly smooth skin. I decided to take it down, and climbed up on the chair.

"Why don't you leave it there?" a voice called out from the direction of the commune. It was Peter.

I froze.

"Isn't that what you want, anyway?" he said.

"The statue is supposed to be a middle-aged woman," I replied, a little lamely.

"I'm not talking about the play," he said in the same flat voice. "If you take it down you're going to have to fight me."

I forced a laugh, but I left the Playboy bunny in place. The idea of fighting with Peter was a joke, for more than one reason. First, Peter was a pacifist, and second, he knew nothing about fighting. I got off the chair and walked toward him.

"Don't be ridiculous," I said. Then, in my most accommodating voice, "What's this all about?"

"You're the ridiculous one," he snarled, assuming an awkward imitation of a fighter's posture. "You can't even see what's happening around you."

"What's to see?" I said, refusing the aggressive gesture by trying to place my hand on his shoulder in comradely fashion.

Peter responded by flattening me with a thoroughly unprofessional sucker-punch. I got to my feet, feeling more rueful than hurt.

"You don't see it, do you?" he screamed. "I've been sleeping with her, you asshole!"

For a split second I wanted to ask who it was he was sleeping with. then the confusion was swept away by total comprehension, which in turn was swept away by blind rage. I attacked wildly, and Peter soon slumped to the ground beneath the hail of my fists.

I stood over him in the pose of Tarzan about to give the victory cry of the wild bull ape, wondering what to do next. The rage I'd felt had vanished as quickly as it had come; Peter was defeated. His face streamed with blood and he was barely conscious. In the cold clarity of victory I knew I had several options: I could kick him, or keep hitting him with my fists, or I could walk away. I walked away. My hand hurt, and my mouth stung where he'd hit me.

Near the house, half hidden by the trees, stood my wife. She'd witnessed the entire scene, and her face was pale and etched with fear.

"Out!" I screamed, with all of Tarzan's volume. "Get away from me!"

She disappeared into the house, and I stormed across the garden to the back door. Then I stopped: I needed a place and some time to think this through. The car keys were in my pocket, and I fished them out and strode purposefully to the garage. I started the car, jammed it into reverse, floored it, slammed on the brakes, cracked it into first, and floored it again. The car fish-tailed noisily down the alley, spitting gravel. But at the corner I stopped. I turned off the motor, slumped back in the seat and stared through the windshield. There was nowhere to go.

I thought for a moment about what I *should* do next. If I were a character in a novel, I could and would commit any of a variety of desperate and dramatic acts: drive the car off a cliff, find Peter and try to bite his ear off or kill him, find my wife and either beat her or beg her forgiveness. Then I thought about Peter, and what he would do. He would, here as in any situation, have to do what I suddenly recognized he'd been doing all his life, and what he would inevitably do for the rest of his life: take one dramatic shot, steal whatever small part of its energy he could, then pack his thin enthusiasms and leave. Life was more than personal ideology, more than just a series of dramatic gestures; it was far more complex than that. Some of it was more interesting, and most of it wasn't. But it was all tactile and material, and it would always see through him and through his arbitrary need to believe. He would be always forced to retreat like the shadow he truly was, having sucked from the world a little bit of its clumsy but delicious sap. No wonder Dostoyevsky hated him so much.

For me, the consequences were more direct and simple: my hand hurt. And as the silent minutes passed, it began to hurt more and more. I tucked it under my arm, started the car and drove carefully and slowly to the hospital.

I'd broken a bone. At the apex of that pure and spontaneous rage, I had not closed my fist.

An hour later I was back in the car, driving home even more carefully. I put the car in the garage, turned off the motor and got out. I still wasn't sure where to go, so I detoured into the garden. The statue was there, almost lost in the branches, and the Playboy fold-out was still tacked onto it. I looked up at the Playboy bunny for a moment, then pulled a leaf from a branch and examined it. The leaf was perfect, green, alive. I crumpled it up, put it into my hip pocket, and walked to the back door, repeating my wife's name over and over. I had no idea what to expect. I'd left a part of myself in the garden, and I had nothing in me with which to face what was ahead except the knowledge that I would never let myself be blinded again.

The Life of Robert Oomer

His life begins as my dream. In the air is a scent both of us have known all our lives, pungent catkins and the muck and ooze of spring break-up. The sun is shining through our familiar haunts, and I feel a long-forgotten impatience awaken in me at the reluctance with which winter lets go its grip.

Through the dirty kitchen window I can see a pickup truck in the driveway, an orange Chevy 4x4. It is splattered with mud. On the windowsill are several plastic pots of sickly African violets, a ring of keys and a glass of water. He turns and gazes into the living room. From here he can't see all of it; only a powder blue couch, a glass coffee table, and on it a heavy glass ashtray halfway in colour between rhinestone and smoke.

I am looking out through the eyes of the man who is seeing these things. What I see is both new and intensely familiar; I know everything this man knows, and I know nothing of it. I look at my hands and arms. They are mine, and they are not mine—larger, more muscled, more damaged by physical labour. I clasp my left wrist in my right hand, a familiar ritual of physical misgiving from having large hands and thin wrists, and it is still the same; it is me. I look up, prepared now to examine the things around me.

A few feet away is a woman, quite tall and striking, with blond hair and blue eyes. I've never seen her before. She is asking me a question, and there is something about the question and her expression that informs me that I am her husband, and that she is my wife. I know this by the way she stands, by the candour of her gaze. She knows who she is and where she is, and her question is casual, proprietary, familiar. I recognize the familiarity without recognizing her: it is situational, and I know the situation. Yet there is something about her that implies a self-containment I've always found attractive in women, a subtle and egoless sense that she is certain of her identity and of the world she is part of. I register, with an instant stab of bitterness, the absence of that quality in the women I've been intimate with, but the bitterness is quickly replaced with guilt—I'm not sure that I'd have understood what it was, had I encountered it.

Why is that quality so visible to me now? This woman has it, and although I've never seen her before this moment, she has known me for at least ten years, almost eight of which we've lived and slept together as man and wife.

It's clearly man-and-wife, and not, say, husband and wife, or partners in marriage. This is a different kind of place from any of the circles I've travelled in, and it is another time. Man-and-wife still make sense in this town, this house, this room I am following her into. It is the bedroom, painted a pastel blue, and it contains a queen size bed covered by a blue bedspread—royal blue velveteen trimmed with gold cord. A part of me is embarrassed: whose taste is this?

The woman continues to talk to me in a matter-of-fact way. She obviously doesn't know what has happened. She thinks I'm the man she's looking at, the one she's loved and been loved by for most of a decade. For a moment I wonder what it's been like, but no, I don't truly want to know, and I don't want to take advantage of what is now happening even though I find her attractive (how could I not?). She *is* attractive in a well-kept, almost raw-boned sort of way: high cheekbones, long straight hair, and probably just over thirty years old. I've *never* seen her face, not anywhere.

She has a strange look in her eyes, probably because I seem a little frightened and confused. It is a clearly protective look. Hmmmm....

"Let's look at the photo albums," I say to her, my voice

reassuringly like my own.

I want to find out what I can of their life together so that I will know a little of what is expected of me. She gets them out (how did I know the albums would be here in this room?) and we sit down on the bed. She hands me one of the albums and I open it.

The photographs confirm what I already suspect. I am at "home", in the small town where I grew up, and which, apparently, I never left. I went to work for my father, maybe, or went from the Forest Service into logging, where the money is. I've done well enough to own a 4x4 and a car (also blue, Japanese, for her?). And a house, full of what, in small town terms, are tasteful furnishings.

I ask the woman careful questions about the people in the photos, trying not to make her suspicious, trying not to let her know I didn't stay, didn't live these ten years with her. I listen carefully to her answers, already relaxed enough to stretch out on the blue bedspread with my knees up. Why not? She stands, walks around the bed and sits again, leaning against my knee, facing me. I stay still, a little tensely now. I haven't earned this intimacy she accords me.

I know most of the people in the snapshots, particularly the ones from the early years of our marriage. Here, though, all the names are different and I enumerate the new names silently, savouring the strange flavours. And I ask her questions, and as she answers them I begin to piece together the story of our life.

I begin to learn who I am. I discover that my surname is Oomer, because that is what, affectionately, she calls me, as if she were in a Mary McCarthy novel. I can't exactly ask her what my first name is, and neither can I take out my wallet in front of her and check the driver's licence. I could, but maybe I don't want to know what kind of wallet it is. After the muddy caulked boots I know are at the back door, the wallet might turn out to be a trucker's wallet with a heavy brass chain attaching it to my belt. And anyhow, my name is Robert. Robert Oomer.

The house we live in is less than two blocks from the house I grew up in. It's at the bottom of a low hill, in what was once a swampy alder thicket. Across the street is the corner store where, as a ten-year-old, I blew a whole winter's paper-route money buying hockey and baseball cards. The house was built about a decade ago (did I build it?) and it has the tacky design and construction common to conventional housing—narrow windowsills, double-glazed aluminum windows, stucco, parquet floors.

It occurs to me that I'm criticizing my surroundings viciously—something in me needs to declare the bad taste, the lack of originality, the tackiness, in order to disqualify any attraction I feel to this life or to the woman I'm looking through this album with, an album in which I'm a stranger in every second or third snapshot.

There are no children of our own in the photographs. That must be a sorrow to her, perhaps even the source of her odd smile. The Dagwood Bumstead in me automatically says we should have had children. Did one of us say no? That's unlikely in this kind of life. Everyone has children here, if they can. Maybe there are no children *here* out of loyalty to the two I have *there.*

I look up at her, and she's smiling again. I feel sorrow for us, and something like guilt. And I watch her mouth as I listen to her tell me half-stories, the unarticulated parts of which are a shared intimacy I know nothing about. It is an elegant mouth, and it reveals a vulnerability I didn't recognize at first.

I want to confess to the masquerade, to beg her forgiveness for not being who I am, but I don't. Instead, I place my hand over hers, touching her long slender fingers....

•

And this is the point at which the ugliness of fiction begins; the point at which as the author of this I'm supposed to take care of my theoretical reader and his or her theoretical needs. And because I've been trained, I have some ideas about what that reader is thinking, and what he or she wants. Some want me to make love to her, thus turning everything into a harlequin reality, and some want me to confess who I am to her, thus turning it into the Twilight Zone, and god knows what others can imagine happening at this point.

I can't do any of those things because they will be untrue. They will be untrue because I would have to invent them. *And I have invented nothing so far in this story.*

To proceed from this point into fiction I would have to invent everything, which I could do either by inventing some sort of dramatic catastrophe, or by analyzing Robert Oomer and his environment and deducing more and more artificial "facts". Whichever I chose, it would almost certainly make me another brute entrepreneur of the imagination, instead of an archaeologist wary of his materials' fragility.

To proceed with the story, the obvious focus of the required manipulations is the woman, whose name, I think, is Linda. Linda Oomer, from Chilliwack, British Columbia, Canada, nee Clapham. We dance a lot at parties, and we dance very well and I am known for having a mean streak when I drink, although never toward her. When Linda has been drinking, she talks dirty, and we don't go out all that much, preferring, on the whole, each other's company. But when we do, watch out, etc....

Is this what anyone wants to know? I doubt it, and besides, it's a violation of the Oomers' lives. The truth is that I simply don't know more.

Still not satisfied? Okay, how about this: Linda Oomer resembles my mother, but with significant improvements. She's taller, slimmer, her breasts are smaller, and she is still sitting on the bed with me, and by now she's probably a little unsettled by my weird behaviour.

By nature she's a confident person, and generally, she's very sure of herself and her position in my life and in our life together. But in the kind of community we live in women still don't have their *own* lives. She is not a separate being, unlike the women who have been important in my other life, etc....

I can't seem to move from this room, with its bedspread of questionable taste, the photo albums full of pictures of myself doing things I've never done. Maybe the story will end here, stranger and wife sitting close to one another on a bed they will never sleep in.

What can I do? The only recourse I have is daydreams, or nightdreams if I'm able. The only facts I can draw on are the facts of a life lived elsewhere, and very differently. I feel badly about abandoning Linda Oomer—predictably, I've fallen in love with her. But I have no practical means of going any further with that or with anything else here, not without moving from pure data (and the traceries of truth in it) to a range of human intelligence where literature, and perhaps life itself, are drowning. I'm talking about invention, commercial or ideological, the true capital of the entrepreneurs.

•

I read somewhere once that "real" imagination is not the ability to invent, but rather the capacity to disclose the most complex nature of that which already exists; be it, as hopefully in this story, from the most obtuse of material data. But making up an ending to this story that would satisfy the expectations of fictive convention would involve techniques that I've come to fear the long-range consequences of using, and which will put me in the same position as a scientist who cooks up data to fit the requirements of the conclusions his method wants him to reach.

And when the most ordinary human life is sufficiently heterogeneous and complex that all attempts to simplify it with conventional paradigms is a gross diminution, why bother?

The life of Robert Oomer is a life I didn't lead but might have. It is like those of people everywhere and like my own. It is complex and it is partial. I don't know if it is coherent to Robert or to Linda, or if they even care whether it is, and I don't know by what means it can be said to be real. I am in the story as I am in the world, trying to locate the source of the grumblings, the whispers and moans, the shouts and the laughter, and hearing the ominous rumble as missiles shift up and down in their silos ready to reinvent all of it forever.

A Personal Memoir of Thomas Carlyle

Thomas Carlyle had a large head. A look at any of those carefully posed photographs shows him bearded and serious, just like all his intellectual contemporaries. In some of the photographs he peers aggressively into the camera; in others he seems to have some difficulty in keeping his great shaggy head from lolling backward or sideways.

The biographers of his day are quick to tell us there are reasons for his ponderous appearance. Carlyle, they repeat over and over, was a man who thought much, studied even more, and felt greatly. When he spoke, his bushy brow bristled and vibrated, and when he walked it was always with stooped shoulders. No wonder. He carried a heavy burden; a stupendous vision of things. Responsibilities of vast import.

Since I was born more than a century after he was, you may already be asking yourself how I am able to write a personal memoir of Carlyle. Well, without meaning to be pedantic, I want you to remember that just as fortrel is not cotton, Art is not Life. Think about that for a minute before you get irritated with me. The shape of Life is determined by the natural manufactures of time and space:

Things like having to go to the bathroom; there's an itch behind your left knee you just have to scratch; now you have to go to the bank and the grocery store; the bathroom again; and when you glance out the window there's a white Chevrolet parked outside your house that you suspect carries either undercover cops or some thieves casing you for an intrusion of some sort. When you get up in the morning you're hungry, or somebody thinks you should be when you're not, and now that itch behind your left knee is after you again.

But in Art, anything can happen. You can be undistracted by those intrusive materialities: you can build perfect symmetries, make sweeping generalities, know ridiculously intimate details of other people's lives. You can act like an irresponsible and capricious asshole—in other words, you can be God.

Carlyle often got himself confused with the Deity, who we all know is famous for confusing Art with Life. Carlyle frequently made it clear that he thought Art was more important than Life, and, if you think about it carefully, it is this opinion of his, more than any of his pronouncements concerning God, that has made him unpopular in our time.

So, Thomas Carlyle was big and mean and pretentious and authoritarian, right? Just like the period of English history he's come to represent. And he had one of those thick patriarchal beards, and spent his free time cruising for hookers, often right after he'd just written an essay about how the moral fibre of the British Empire needed to be strengthened and how prostitution was a smudge on the nation and people ought to stop whacking off and so forth. Most of us know the imagery. Somewhere close to the centre of this imagery, at least in current academic opinion, lies the career and writing of Thomas Carlyle.

Sometimes, less polite things are said. Just yesterday the well-educated, extensively psychoanalyzed wife of a friend flicked an errant ladybug from her camel-hair suit and told me that, personally, she would never forgive Carlyle for being the Father of Fascism.

Actually, her views on Carlyle and his time, like those of the mainstream biographers (now mostly dead), contain some inaccuracies. It *is* true that Carlyle's thought was often reactionary and that he referred to black people by names that have been out of fashion since 1957. It is also true that in 1850, 80,000 of London's 800,000 citizens were prostitutes. It is a fact that women of the time had three choices open to them if they were not wealthy: they could marry, they could become domestic servants, or they could sell their asses. It is also a fact that most males lived lives of thorough ambivalence, so much so that sleeping with one's own wife for the sheer erotic mammalian pleasure of it was an oddity. A man bred his children with his spouse, but for pleasure most men went off to a brothel. There was, at the core of the society, something foul.

Did you know that when Queen Victoria died the attending morticians who prepared her body for burial discovered, in its most private reaches, one of the most truly astonishing infestations of crab lice ever seen? The vermin were reportedly so numerous and large that the infestation was estimated to be of at least fifteen years' duration. One is left to calculate the degree of suffering and misery that went on beneath those vast, dark, and formal skirts of the Empire.

•

Thomas Carlyle also suffered a great deal. He didn't have crabs; he had stomach problems and domestic troubles. That may alter the presumed causality of the stooped shoulders I noted at the beginning of this story: perhaps he wasn't hunched over because of the heavy moral and intellectual burdens he carried. Perhaps he was doubled up because something was gnawing at his guts.

Two more details concerning his physique should be added to the portrait I began with. First, Carlyle only acquired his patriarchal Victorian beard late in life and then only by artifice. He had no natural beard. He wore a false one. And during the last twenty or so years of his life he spent roughly two hours a day with it: an hour gluing it on each morning and an hour removing it again each night. Second, Thomas Carlyle was a dead ringer for D.H. Lawrence. The two men might have been brothers—twins even—had Lawrence not been born more than eighty years after Carlyle.

Unfortunately, Lawrence and Carlyle were never able to speak with one another. Just think of the delight they might have taken with one another in conversation.

A brief note about D.H. Lawrence is in order. There are some unusual circumstances pertaining to the life of Lawrence that provide important clues to Carlyle's real personality. For instance, Lawrence wasn't much of a boxer. As a matter of fact he lost every fist fight he ever engaged in, and he had an unusual number of fights during his career, most of them with Frieda, whose uppercut he never learned to avoid. His most famous fight, curiously, was one that never actually took place. Ernest Hemingway, having heard of Lawrence's many losses to Frieda, once challenged him to a three-round exhibition. Hemingway was desperate for a win at the time, and sought to take advantage of Lawrence's smaller physical stature and minimal skills. Lawrence declined the bout as politely as he could on the grounds that he was about to die of consumption.

I don't want this to be taken as mere gossip. My point is that Carlyle was a small and rather delicate man, just like D.H. Lawrence; a man with stomach ulcers who got beaten up by his wife and couldn't grow a beard. But he didn't have crab lice. He was a great rhetorician and a great thinker, and as I got to know him better I grew to like him. He wasn't at all like the biographers portrayed him in the days when his thought was still fashionable.

As for D.H. Lawrence, I haven't had the pleasure of knowing him personally. It was strictly his writing that counted with me. Maybe it's because the contradictions in him are too blurry, too streamlined by his polemical interests—and too current—for there to be much chance of my breaking past his projections in a face-to-face encounter. What he wanted was a kind of polymorphous sexual experience of the world that's actually very common these days. If I were to wake him up and tell him that most of my generation has had what he so craved, that it doesn't satisfy our cosmological urges, and that it leads, instead, to a lot of selfish interpersonal anarchy and solitary individualism, he'd probably be hurt and disappointed. We're in the middle of his dream, and I don't want to wake him until I'm a little clearer on what it is that we are supposed to awaken to.

•

"A man—pardon me, a human being," Carlyle told me in our very first conversation, "must have a coherent world. By that I mean a physical coherence—a city—if he, or she as the case now is, is to produce any wisdom deeper than tactics or what you call street-smarts. The metropolis, the megalopolis, which has instead of structure and coherence a series of interdependent and interpenetrating systems that function with only the barest of short-term efficiencies, does not provide that coherent world. It has produced a history that is really just a rubbish heap of fulfilled but pointless personal ambitions."

"Then why did you spend all those years in London?" I asked. "Weren't you in fact pursuing personal ambition, marshalling what we now call guru power?"

He shifted in his chair and appeared to be uncomfortable. I spotted it, and on an instinct offered him a tagamet tablet.

"Try this," I said. "It's a recent medical advance that actually does help."

Carlyle glanced at it, popped it into his mouth and swallowed it without ceremony.

"I made a mistake," he continued with a sigh. "And by the time I was through blaming all the wrong things for my misery—my wife Jane, my physical constitution, the rampant Mammonism of the so-called democrats—I was addicted to the power I'd gained. But I never pretended to be God."

"You just acted as if you had his ear, right?"

Carlyle scowled at me without speaking. His scowl, I quickly learned, was an almost physical force. I adjusted my statement.

"Okay, you didn't really believe you were God. But let's go back a little, here, and look at some of the things you said that remain contentious. Does God love good citizens?"

"Does *who* love *what*?" he demanded, peering at me with renewed irritability.

I repeated the phrase, and the second time around it sounded silly. "Does God love good citizens?"

"First of all, lad, there is no God! And second, how should I know the answer to that?" His irritable expression suddenly dissolved in a grin. "Oh! That! I didn't say that. That was a simplifying vilification of those blasted journalists. You must return to the opus in detail. To interpret my proposals for society on that kind of basis is a little like reading the Bible and deciding that all it means is 'kiss everyone'."

He shifted in his chair again.

"The public realm in my time," he continued, "as in yours, was fabricated from personal ambition, covert greed, outright lies and vulgarizations of once-effective institutions. I sought to rebuild the lexicon of perception in a way that would expose those vulgarities and afford a rebirth of a cultured naivety. I failed, because Mr. Marx interposed with an irrefutable economic analysis that the masses—and I daresay most of the intellectuals—mistook for a new religion."

I must have looked puzzled, because Carlyle abruptly reached across the table and gently bounced his fist off my forehead as if determining whether or not it was made of wood.

"Within the mechanics of the Marxist canon, my dear boy, is a messianism that Marx and Engels took no trouble to hide in their letters, and which declared its toxicity soon after the first State organized itself around it."

"Remember," he said, covering his mouth with one hand to release a deep but muted belch, "I said that human beings are facing three hundred years of revolution—it would have been more accurate to call it a convolution, actually, because revolution means you're only turning the wheel. All revolution demands is the transfer of power, not a transformation of it."

He looked up at me to see if I'd understood, and as he did, his expression changed from resolute concentration to intense discomfort. He looked as if he had an aircraft propellor rotating in his stomach, and the attached plane was thundering down the runway.

"Do you have another of those tablets?" he asked. "That one didn't seem to help."

I reached over to my jacket, removed another tablet from the vial in the pocket, and handed it to him. He smiled wanly and popped it into his mouth. There was a deep rumbling from his stomach and he lifted one buttock slightly. I heard a distinct hissing.

"Can we go into a bit more detail about what you called 'cultured naivety'?" I asked, getting up from my chair to look for my cigarettes.

I'd left them on a table near the door, and when I went over to get them a distinctly visible cloud of fetid air tracked me. I lit a cigarette and tried to use the smoke to mask the foulness around me as I walked back to my chair and sat down. The air there had cleared slightly.

(I was later to learn that Carlyle's gastric effusions had a mind of their own, attacking anyone who tried to escape from them. When our acquaintanceship grew more intimate, Carlyle told me that from mid-career these apparently self-motile clouds were the secret behind his reputation as a brilliant conversationalist. He'd let one out in a roomful of distracted or rude listeners, and while he spoke the cloud would hover just above the heads of his terrified audience for as long as fifteen minutes, waiting for someone foolish enough to attempt an escape. As time went on he learned to renew the cloud as often as needed, and thereby held his audiences transfixed.)

"Cigarette?" I asked, safe in my chair.

"No thanks. Listen. Would you mind if I removed this infernal beard?"

"Go right ahead," I said. "They're no longer required, you know. Men only wear them now to cover acne scars or weak chins."

"It's pleasant to know that civilization has made a few advances," he sighed, getting up from his chair.

He disappeared into the washroom for the better part of an hour, and I used the time to take a nap. While I slept, I had an interesting dream, but it has nothing to do with this story. I awoke to find a refreshed and remarkably youthful-looking Thomas Carlyle, prodding at me.

"You asked about cultured naivety," he said. "There is much to say about it."

"There is indeed," I agreed, unconsciously mimicking his speech mannerisms and accent. "It's an attractive and dangerous concept. I hope it can climb atop the old saying 'a little learning is a dangerous thing' without falling on its fuzzy face."

Carlyle darkened instantly. "I hope you're not making fun of my lack of facial hair," he snapped.

"No, not at all," I replied, realizing what my clumsy attempt at imitation had gotten me to say. "If you haven't noticed, I've got the same problem."

He peered at me with a new kind of interest. "Yes," he said, stroking his chin, "I see you have. Well. Not the problem for you it was for me."

"It has been at times. While I was a teenager it caused some grief."

"Teenager?"

"A commercial expression for an artificially-created consumer bracket. It means the same thing as adolescence."

Carlyle snorted with laughter. "Poor lad. At least you're not Scottish."

"What's Scotland got to do with this?" I asked.

"I was raised near the Scottish border. Do you know how brutal the Scots can be about beards? A man's future is determined by the scale of one's beard. Since I had none, I was forced to leave the only home I ever cared for to live in the swarmeries of vile London, and then, perpetually in mufti. I hated English food, I hated the unctuous democracy of the rich, I hated the rampant Mammonism that swept the poor before it like chaff on the wind...."

"This doesn't quite make sense," I said, deliberately interrupting his effusion of rhetoric before it reached gale force.

Carlyle collapsed into his chair.

"I'm sorry," he said with unexpected humbleness. "Sometimes when I talk the rage escapes. All my life, I was hostage to my own ambitions. I had appetites that nothing seemed to satisfy. Most of all, I was in exile from my own heart and hearth."

"I didn't realize," I said, taken aback by his sincerity. "I know a little about being an exile. This is a civilization of exiles. I too come from a place that I loved deeply but was forced by cultural circumstances to leave, and I've lived with unsatisfied appetites ever since. Not as long as you lived with them, of course."

A spasm stiffened him for a second, and he stared at the floor. When it passed, his momentary depression seemed to depart with it.

"Tell me what it is you don't understand," he said in a gentle voice.

"I think you answered it. Please go on with what you were telling me."

"About cultured naivety?"

"Yeah. Quite frankly I have a lot of doubts about returning to any kind of naive condition, but there's something attractive about putting 'culture' and 'naivety' together. What do you mean by 'culture'? I assume you don't mean it in the neutral sense of 'culture' being the descriptive sum of a society's social, political and interpersonal procedures."

"No. Nor do I mean it as that collection of arcane specialities the wealthy use to dress themselves in mental finery and intimidate everyone else by fostering the belief that politics and art will always be incomprehensible and beyond most people's means. And of course you have doubts about it. I had doubts in my own time about what universal literacy would produce if there were no corollary commitments to social justice. As a liberal, you have sought the universalization of a nurturing culture in your time, just as we fought for universalization of literacy in mine. The sad fact is that in both eras the result has been the same: literacy and culture became commodities to be competed for. That in itself isn't bad. What is bad, and what was not predicted, is that *generalization* occurred instead of universalization, and the energy of both literacy and culture—as social forces leading to social justice and moral density—was sapped."

"Moral density?"

"Literacy and culture are only meaningful if they contribute to the individual's capacity to make informed and disinterested social, political and personal decisions. Ideally, and pragmatically, democracy must lead to that condition in the individual. And I stress the word 'must'. Excuse me if I use the vocabulary of your Psychology here, but the key to a healthy society is the avoidance of pathology. Pathology is created, however you examine it, and in whatever context, by too narrow a definition of self-interest: be it the body's 'need' for a given stimulant, like alcohol, or the mind's 'need' for power or pleasure. Your mental therapists counsel balance, but that is only part of the elixir—the medium of it, one might say. The other part—the substantive content, is moral density, which is the product of training and methodological experience within a body of complex knowledge. The social and political applications of moral density—at any level within a society, are obvious."

My head was spinning, but Carlyle seemed transformed. He sat straighter in his chair, and the pain that had clouded his expression earlier was no longer there. His eyes now darted toward me with each new idea, and his hands rolled and twisted in the air as he spoke as if he were forming and positioning each concept.

"The basis of democracy, as Plato understood completely, was education and universalization. When it is not, the result will be

Mammonism in the public realm, and the kind of pathological individualism your age has achieved."

"I'm still unclear on much of what you're saying," I mumbled apologetically. "Can you talk a little bit more about how universality is different from generality?"

"Universalization is dynamic," he said. "It breeds no levelling absolutes, but rather activates ideas in order to transform material conditions. In the public realm, it generates discourse, never, as your epoch has been taught to believe, sleep. The best signal of political health is the amount and quality of debate that goes on in the streets."

"We seem to have a great deal of street-debate," I objected. "It rarely becomes coherent."

"Don't be too quick to judge," he cautioned. "The actions of any collective are the most difficult of all things to see accurately. You have to see through yourself in order to understand them, and that is a difficult thing: you become invisible in order to see the real visibility."

"Huh?"

"Visibility is the consequence of individual values working within the collective. Values are irrelevant unless they work on the street."

"Shouldn't those values work at the hearth first?"

"Don't be sentimental," Carlyle snapped. "The family—direct genetic kinship—had already been seen through in my time as an economically manipulated structure that saps intelligence and social energy. The twentieth century should have learned to move toward kinship structures that offer positive energies instead of allowing intelligence to be bled by loyalties that are not tied directly to enlarging understanding."

I experienced the strange sensation of being ashamed of my world.

"Don't waste your time with such an unproductive emotion," Carlyle said, reading my mind. I looked startled.

"Of course I can read your mind," he smiled, again reading my thoughts. "If you think about it for a moment you'll know why."

He didn't give me any time to think about it, though.

"Because your time has not learned to work with the mass nature of intellectual reality," he went on. "Instead of peaceful streets in which informed citizens engage in earnest discourse, you have demonstrations—mobs engaged in sectarian imperialisms. You have forgotten that ideas are the doors to social justice. They are not pickets against conversation. The formulation of slogans signals the closure of public discourse and little else. Their presence is an unfailing indication of social pathology."

"You sound like Leon Trotsky," I said. "That's what he wanted."

"His followers wanted something else," Carlyle replied dryly.

He rose from his chair and walked to the window. Across the street, two of my neighbours were arguing across the chainlink fence that separated their properties. I knew exactly what it was they were arguing about: one of them, an avid gardener, uses the fence to grow climbing roses, a red variety that blooms around midsummer in small and extremely fragrant profusion. The other neighbour habitually prunes the rose bush wherever he feels the vines impinge on his property, often cutting main stems—as he claims, by accident. Carlyle watched them argue for a moment before he turned back to me.

"You recall that I said that humanity was at the beginning of a revolution that would take 300 years to complete."

It was a statement, not a question. He was now a silhouette in the window-frame, and I watched him tug at the beard that was no longer there.

"Your society," he said carefully, "has now reached the fulcrum crisis in that revolution."

Still in silhouette, he doubled over as he spoke, as if the crisis he referred to had fallen on his shoulders with enormous force. A low moan issued from his very core. I guessed that the aircraft propeller had started up once more. I touched his shoulder.

"Perhaps we should stop for a moment," I said, "and try something else. I'm having trouble deciphering who is saying what in this story, and if I'm confused, I'm sure the reader is. We'll come back to it. If we keep going as we are, my editor is going to demand some plot action."

"As you wish," said Carlyle, more agreeably than I would have expected. "A story can't be all discourse, I suppose, or the relationship between language and concept will lose its transparency. If that happens, the fiction dissolves, and the reader will starve on the meagre fare of conventional discourse."

"That's semiotics!" I yelped. "You can't know anything about that stuff."

"No," he admitted, "but you can."

"I'd rather not," I mumbled.

•

It is late afternoon, August 14, 1838. Under the looming conical canopies of dark sycamores that trail down from the piney uplands surrounding Balmoral Castle, one might see a solitary figure walking. And one does! She is a young woman of perhaps twenty summers, returning to the castle alone, along a pathway of soft needles. In her gloved hand is a small bouquet of wildflowers. She is a small woman, fair-haired and robust, and despite her wide and cumbersome skirts she moves with an alert, carefree preoccupation.

One might also note, looking more carefully, a slightly built man in his early forties propped against one of the sycamores. And there he is—not so much resting as crouching. Doubled over. Judging from his expression, he is in some internal agony, but there is no panic in his eyes. He is evidently familiar with his affliction. There is a light knapsack on his back, and, from a distance, one could take him for a hunchback.

Glancing up, the young woman spots him and stops. She believes that what she sees *is* a hunchback. But instead of being afraid, she is curious. This is, after all, nineteenth-century Scotland, not New York in the 1980s. With a characteristic twist of her hips that sends her rigid crinolines into chaos, she strides toward the presumed hunchback.

"Sir," she says, the imperiousness of her self-confidence undone by the tonal sweetness of her voice. "I thought you a cripple. Announce yourself and your intentions."

"Madam," replies the man in a rich voice thatched by the faint hint of a Scottish accent that makes his words sound like heather brushing along a skein of velvet, "I am a poor scrivener on a summer ramble. I have not the slightest notion where I am, and therefore no better idea of where I'm bound."

"William?" asks the young woman. "Are you William?"

"William who?" asks the man."

"William Wordsworth," says she, already disappointed.

"Do I look to be a man of sixty-eight?" he replies crossly. "Wordsworth is spending the summer at Durham. My name is Thomas Carlyle, late of London. What is yours?"

"I will call you 'Quasimodo'," she giggles. "You may call me 'Victoria'. Can't you stand upright?"

"So mysterious you are, young madam," answers Carlyle, straightening his posture as well as he can. "I suppose you are Victoria, Monarch of the Realm."

"As you wish, sir," she laughs musically. "And this is my castle, ancient Balmoral."

"Queen Victoria you might well be," he chuckles, "but this is *not* Balmoral. This spot must be twenty miles from the castle estate, by my reckoning."

"Have your world as you prefer," says the young woman. "But do rest awhile, and we can talk. I rarely have anyone to talk to these days."

•

"Is that what you call naturalism?" Carlyle asked me when I showed him a draft of the passage you've just read.

"Yeah. It would lead to that if I went on much further with it. Using the present tense is already a problem because it restricts my ability to comment indirectly on the action. If I used third person past tense it would become even easier to shape the reader's perception."

"It's worse than Dickens," he shuddered. "If anything, it's more time-wasting and presumptive. I would have thought that, as democracy advanced, it would undermine the manipulative artistic conventions that developed in my era. Instead, they appear to have become all-pervasive."

"Democracy didn't advance, as you've already pointed out. It merely generalized. The way in which that has infected the writing of prose fiction is to make the narrator absolutely invisible—as you point out, more so than in Dickens. So the operational intelligence of the reader has no way of making contact with the narration. The built-in pre-condition—that the reader accept, on faith, the fantasy-premise of omniscient narration—ensures that the reader will always be no more than a passive spectator."

"To be sure, faith always ensures stasis. Has no one attacked the political implications of this procedure?"

"Not until recently, and then without real popular success. For a long time most of those who attempted to blow the whistle have been classified as 'experimental' and 'difficult', and they've been given high-paying jobs teaching in universities to ensure that they won't have the energy or the economic incentive to really pursue new procedures."

"I'm still unclear about how these experimental energies are stifled."

"For the last thirty years there has been enough wealth available to buy off all serious protest against the alienating structure of the political and economic systems. Much of the theoretical protest has been bought off and ghetto-ized within the university system. Literature—what is now ironically referred to as *serious* literature, has been almost entirely funnelled off to university-confined hobbyists."

"No one has objected?"

"No one saw what it was. It seemed, on the surface, to be legitimate recognition. It seemed to offer the opportunity to study and work at leisure, and to rise above a life of material poverty. Recently, as the public wealth dwindles, the leisure has been reduced, and the people who were taken in by this process woke up to find that they are now economically dependent on a system that is increasingly less tolerant of them. It's still going on—accelerating, actually. And many of the victims are finding out that they want the comforts of a reasonable income more than they want the leisure to study and think."

"Never mind the fate of willing addicts," Carlyle said. "What has become of those who have attempted to combat this trend?"

"It's complicated. Because bourgeois life has successfully encouraged a methodological separation between public and private activity—at both the conceptual and pragmatic levels—and because a similar separation is made between intellectual and emotional experience, most writers apply their 'experimental' impulses insurgently, within their private emotional comprehensions, and within the politically acceptable subject matter of private emotion."

Carlyle was astonished. "They're encouraged to do this?"

"Not much of the encouragement is direct. But the economic rewards are set up so that the less serious you are the more money you can make. And if you insist on working with ultimate questions, you face a kind of friendly contempt from all sides, even from your academic allies."

"*Who* is it that does all this?" he demanded peevishly. "Is there a visible oligarchy, or a specific group of conspirators that consciously carries out these vile manipulations?"

"I don't think there's any coherent conspiracy, or a specific group of conspirators. There doesn't need to be. The operation of capital creates its energy by fostering conflict, and by blocking the conduits between public and private life. By artificially separating emotional and intellectual information, and by strictly determining their social uses, the system makes itself invisible inside the smoke-screen of regulated dissent. It is as invisible to those who benefit from it as it is to its victims. It becomes morally invisible, and breaks down what you've called the moral density of individuals, such that all they can operate from is an extremely private and narrow definition of self-interest. Thus, the manipulation is largely self-inflicted."

"As are all successful forms of slavery. Have you thought about how to reverse your slavery?"

I hadn't, to this point, included myself in the calculation.

"In Art, or in Life?" I replied.

Carlyle brushed my witticism aside. "You're an artist. Obviously you should work within the range of your knowledge. You should do your primary work as an artist."

"The problem I have is knowing where to work, and how. Even as an artist, I'm confronting a hydra."

A thin smile rippled the surface of his visage without altering its severity and without reaching his eyes, which remained opaque with concentration.

"Has it occurred to you that you may be facing a new non-material life-form?"

"A new god? What we're facing is the evolution of capital. That's all I'm sure of. I don't see how it is helpful to think of it as a life-form."

The great brow furrowed in a now-familiar expression. "Look at it again," he said. "You may be missing the most obvious clues. As you know, I've always believed that life *is* intelligence. Twentieth century cybernetics tells us that the characteristic that indicates intelligence is the capacity to redefine and utilize feedback. In the nineteenth century, capital could not do that. It operated mechanically, with the single impulse to expand industrial processes and widen the margin between subsistence and labour productivity—in other words, pretty much as Marx described it. Its ability to diversify those processes through automation has obviated the human part of the labour formula. This has buried Marxism as a political alternative in the twentieth century. For some years now citizens have been more important as consumers than as producers, and in the most recent metamorphosis capitalism seems to be bent on breaking the importance of even the consumers of industrial production."

"Really?" I said, unable to assimilate what he was saying, and content to wait for some later opportunity to study his theorizings at leisure.

"Yes, really," he replied, his eyebrows arching sarcastically.

•

Eight days passed before Thomas Carlyle discovered the true identity of his young acquaintance. Four of those days, the nineteenth through the twenty-second of August 1838, are a blank in the annals of English royal history, one of the few that exists since the Reformation. They are also a blank in the records that remain of the life of Thomas Carlyle.

The royal log at Balmoral castle for August 14th notes that twenty-year-old Queen Victoria, crowned less than three months previously on June 28th, returned from an unattended stroll on the castle grounds some four hours later than expected, and that on her return, she was tired but extremely cheerful. The log displays no anxiety with her late return, perhaps because the castle staff were familiar with the young queen's carelessness with time, and her independence generally. Europe was then at peace, and there was no thought that the young free spirit might have been in danger.

For the next four days, the entries in the castle log are patterned if not routine: long walks daily from early afternoon to early evening. Then on the nineteenth, the log entry is missing, as are the entries until the twenty-third, for which day it is recorded, simply, that the 'situation is calm'. We are given no inkling of the 'situation' from which the turbulence has been removed, and the only evidence of change, aside from the missing entries for these four days, is a change in the handwriting. Someone new was now keeping the log.

•

When I asked Carlyle to recount his side of the events of those eight days, he stared at me solemnly—an expression, I learned, that often appeared when he was trying to stifle one of his many inner impulses. He giggled, and began the recounting with the words 'Once upon a time', then immediately dissolved into uncontrolled laughter. This odd sequence was repeated several times before he was able to calm himself.

"It's just that all the conventions available for describing biographical and autobiographical information are those of romantic fiction. In order to make purely factual information comprehensible to your audience, you have to dress it up as if it were untrue—or at the very least informationally twisted— and fraught with symbolic references. What's so funny is that this particular set of facts doesn't have any larger frame of reference, despite the involvement of the queen of England. The entire episode is dumb fact; it is savagely, profanely factual."

He tried to begin the story several more times without succeeding.

"Why don't we tell the story, or outline the facts, in the form of an interview," I suggested. "That way we can create the illusion of on-the-spot fact-giving, and at the same time obtain the fictionalizing illusion of dialogue. You can rewrite all your answers afterward if you want to. It's called 'cooking an interview'. Everyone does it."

•

Brian Fawcett (BF): When you first encountered the young woman who called herself Victoria, and when you joked with her about being the queen, did you suspect that she might in fact be the queen?

Thomas Carlyle (TC): No. (pause) Oh. I get the idea. (clears throat) I could see that she was well bred, and that she might be either English or German, judging from her accent. What would have thrown me off, as your text suggests, is that I thought I was some miles away from where I was. I knew that I was in the general vicinity of Balmoral, but I thought it was some distance further, and I was unaware of the distance I'd walked in the previous days. When she informed me of her identity and our location, I assumed that she was joking on both counts. Because I was lost, and because I was, uh, coming up from an attack of cramps that, in retrospect, certainly had something to do with the extra distance I walked, I, uh....

(There is a crash in the background—a motor vehicle accident.)

BF: What is it?

(An interval as Carlyle goes to the window, chuckles briefly, then returns.)

TC: Two of the penis-shaped automobiles seem to have collided. Is that what they're for?

BF: Camaros?

TC: Yes.

BF: Are they for what? Collisions or genital extensions?

TC: Collisions.

BF: I don't know. (slightly irritated) Can we go on with the interview? What did you do after that first encounter?

TC: I beg your pardon?

BF: The first afternoon you met Victoria...where did you go after she left, and what did you do? (Sirens are audible in the distance.)

TC: The young woman and I talked until dusk, and then I walked to an inn some two miles hence, and she returned to Balmoral. (pause) Before we go any further, I'm confused. Do I speak, in this interview, as if all the details are known and are in the past tense, or do I sustain suspense by speaking only in terms of the information I've revealed?

BF: (pause, with rustling noises) I...er...I'm not sure. I suppose everything is known theoretically to both of us, but it's impossible and probably presumptuous to calculate the understanding of the reader. (muted) *There's one hovering over my head.*

TC: (also muted) *It will dissipate. Just don't fidget.*

(The sirens reach a crescendo, drowning out speech, and are suddenly silent. The opening and closing of car doors can be heard in the background.)

BF: When did you discover that the encounter took place on the grounds of Balmoral castle?

TC: That's a rather stupid question. I found out that evening at the inn, of course.

BF: So at what point, uh, did you suspect that the young woman might be the Queen?

TC: I still didn't suspect, although perhaps I might have. You're assuming that the comings and goings of the Royal Family were as carefully scrutinized then as they are today. But you're forgetting that in 1838 we didn't have your silly tabloids drawing sensational conclusions each time a royal personage went to the toilet.

BF: I'm not sure what you mean.

TC: What I mean is that even though I happened to be on the property of one of a number of royal residences, there was no reason for me to think that the attractive but commonly dressed young woman I met would be the Queen herself.

BF: What was next? (There is a crash) Dammit!

TC: We met at the same spot on each of the next four days. You haven't harmed yourself, have you?

BF: No, I'm fine. The arm on this damned chair is curved, and every time I put something on it, it falls off. Did you and she meet by mutual agreement?

TC: Not the next day. Both of us, by happy accident, were strolling near the same spot at the same time. After that second encounter, we planned our trys—er, meetings.

BF: You fell in love with her, didn't you? Without knowing or caring who she was. You fell in love with her and the two of you spent four days at the inn together.

TC: We embarked on a long and complex friendship, yes. As to whether or not we spent four days at the inn as lovers, I don't see that it is any of your concern, nor is it related in any way to the concerns of this story.

BF: Let's tie down a few more facts, then. At what point did you realize that the girl Victoria was Queen Victoria?

TC: On the afternoon of August 22nd.

Our interview ended there, because Carlyle got up and left the room. When he returned twenty minutes later, he was pale and withdrawn. I asked if he felt up to finishing the interview, and he said no, he did not feel up to it, and that he had said all he intended to about the matter. Furthermore, he asked me to erase the cassette tape on which I'd recorded the interview, and took some trouble to ensure that I complied with his request. By happy accident, I erased another cassette, and thus have been able to transcribe the interview in precise detail.

•

Several days later Carlyle interrupted me while I was working.

"I have some questions to ask you," he said, in a way that let me know I lacked the authority to refuse.

"Okay," I agreed, reluctantly. "You're my guest here, and I'm trying my best to be accommodating."

He brushed my attempt at politeness aside with an impatient gesture. "I want to question you about the sub-text of this story. I don't see how it relates to the larger subject matter in your book, which, you say, is capital."

"Yes."

"Then let me start with my understanding of the word: capital means wealth. Or, at least, wealth that is being used to create and perpetuate wealth."

I must have looked startled, because Carlyle made an awkward lunge across the table we were sitting at and caught me by the lapels of my jacket. He pulled me nose to nose, in a gesture that was as theatrical as it was out of character.

"You don't even know what the word means, do you?" he hissed.

"I do know what it means, or at least what it used to mean. It defines the part of the proceeds or product of a productive process that remains after the subsistence needs of the labourer or labourers required to produce it have been met."

"That's very abstract. What about the cost of materials, taxes, debt, service and insurance charges on equipment and so forth? Aren't you forgetting those? And what about the other meanings of the word?"

"Like what?"

" 'Capital' has a number of meanings that should interest you. First of all, it can mean, simply, 'relating to the head,' or, 'affecting, or involving loss of the head or life.' It also means that which is punishable by death, or, if you're speaking of an enemy, you might call him 'capital' if he or she were a deadly or mortal enemy. A non-Marxist and arcane definition of 'capital' is 'of or pertaining to the original funds of a trader or company' hence serving as a basis for financial or other operations.' In other words, it means 'accumulated wealth'—authority and power."

"I try to make it mean 'publicly inaccessible surplus value'. But many of your definitions are entertaining."

"I wasn't trying to be Punchinello," Carlyle said, obviously irritated with my attitude. "I want to make you aware that the word you keep jabbing at me is loaded with rhetoric and cross-definitions."

"Yes, but we're getting bogged down. What we need to discuss is how capital operates now, outside of abstraction and history."

He rose from his chair and walked to the window, gently massaging his stomach. "Look across the street," he said. "That's how it's working."

My two neighbours had been at it again. A carpenters' crew had been working in the rose-growing neighbour's yard for the past two days constructing a solid eight-foot high fence. The fence was finished, and now the carpenters were building sturdy trellises for the vines. Unfortunately, the best of the rose plants had been destroyed during the building of the fence.

"What they're doing is only a sociological metaphor," I snapped, "and not a very accurate one at that. You've been bitching about the sentimentalizing conventions of fiction, and here you are participating in the sort of stupid nonsense that modern fiction is filled with. This little miracle play across the street is nothing but a modern private argument over property, and whatever deeper meaning it may have it is cross-referenced so heavily by idiosyncratic data that it's opaque. Let's go back to the implications of what you said earlier: that capital might be a new life-form."

Instead of arguing as I'd expected, Carlyle settled back in his chair, seemingly ready to listen.

"I'm going to start from a Marxist base," I said, "because it offers the only available systematic view of capital, and of its phenomena. The first thing I note about it is that Marx's definition is an idealized one. Even in his time, those who controlled the means of production produced as great a profit as possible without regard for the subsistence needs of the labouring masses. In that sense, capital is just a dirty idea dirtied further by the world. More interesting, though, is what it implies: that the dynamic of capital lies elsewhere, in less tangible concepts."

"Like wealth, you mean," Carlyle interjected.

"Yes. The dynamic always involves privilege and the withholding of valued materials."

"You're missing something. Since the French Revolution discovered the political value of fear, ruling factions have kept the lower echelons in a state of anxiety. During the French Revolution it was called 'Terror'. I don't know what it's called now, but I'm sure it's present in any of your political formulations."

"For the proletariat the terror was subsistence," I replied. "When automation, and other technological improvements to the industrial process obviated the proletariat, the Terror changed. Human labour is no longer the vital ingredient for the creation of capital. In many cases, it isn't even necessary. Following from the changed equation, the class that once lived by selling their labour—the working class—

now lives by consuming. That is their political and economic justification. They compete now, not in order to obtain subsistence, but to be able to consume in a conspicuous way. But more interesting than that, is the way that, as the complexity of the class system grows, capital devises an appropriate form of Terror for each of the classes. For what used to be the working class, and for the lower levels of the middle class, the Terror is the terror of not being able to consume conspicuously. For intellectuals, and perhaps for the petty bourgeoisie in general, the Terror is not being able to secure oneself within a structure of commonly agreed definitions and meaning, and of finding oneself unable to apply one's values in any practical way."

"You mean that one is unable to consume them."

"Yes. That is another way of putting it."

"Let's look at this in a different way," Carlyle said, with the glee of a mathematician confronting an interesting new problem. "What, then, is the substance or thing that is being withheld? And is it the true image of wealth?"

"Wealth?"

"Yes. Wealth is always that which is perceived to be in short supply by the mass of people, and those who are considered wealthy always express their wealth in an exaggerated characterization of this image of wealth. Prior to the 19th century in England, for instance, wealth was expressed in terms of food—the rich held banquets that were vast, sumptuous and deliberately wasteful. But as agricultural methods improved, as population increased and moved to the city, the perceived image of wealth shifted to what then became scarce—decent housing. And sure enough, my century is characterized by the idiotic mansions of the newly wealthy."

"You're right. And the ridiculous banquets disappear."

"There were banquets," Carlyle said, with some distaste. "But they were subsidiary to the real displays of wealth: the halls the banquets were served in."

"And in my time?"

"What's in short supply now is obvious: reliable information. Just as the 19th century was characterized by a preoccupation with housing, your time is marked by its fascination with information. There's so much information around that, to the average intelligent citizen, it's impossible to sort out. Hence, there is a widespread belief that there are sources of secret and reliable information and that only the privileged have access to them—the occult truth movements of the 1960s, or the insiders' economic newsletters of the 1980s are examples."

"But the modern situation seems completely different. Most information is public—much of our legal system is aimed at ensuring equitable access to it. Nobody is starving or living on the street, as it were."

"Look closer," Carlyle said, gravely, "and you will see that the situation is identical. The image of wealth is a fetish, and takes the form of whatever the given society is expending its most inventive energies on. The information that is publicly available now is like unused farmland in the 18th century or stacked stone and wood in the 19th. An ordinary citizen has no more chance of using today's information than a peasant in a turnip field had to use the land 200 years ago."

"The controlling classes don't know how to use information, either," I said.

"They don't need to use it. That is never their intention. They want only the aura of power it offers as a fetish, and to withhold that aura from everyone else. That is the social pathology of wealth."

"This doesn't explain capital."

"Not if you insist on seeing capital as an oligarchy of fat men in tall hats and black suits. The 'capitalists' are as much in power in the communist states as they are here. They simply control the wealth of the nation more abstractly. Since personal material wealth is 'illegal', controlling money as a commodity is less important than controlling people. Authority and power become the equivalent capital commodities to possess, use and to withhold from others. You still aren't taking the reality of modern wealth apart. You're still relying on an image of it that has been dead for 300 years. Wealth does not mean *plenty*. It means control, and the rancorous *withholding* of plenty."

•

"What did you think about Albert?" I asked Carlyle in a relaxed moment a few hours later.

"Who?"

"Prince Albert, the Royal Consort. Didn't Victoria marry him less than two years after you met her?"

"Boring man, really," Carlyle said, still preoccupied by our earlier discussion. "A terrible dilettante. He had no faults—never drank or smoked or much of anything. But he had no passions either. The only time anyone ever saw the man with his dander up was in 1942 when he was disposing of Melbourne and Baron Stockmar. He seemed to have decided that both of them were threats to his control over Victoria. God knows what set that off. She never spoke of it, except to express her distaste for the Baron."

"He produced nine children. That indicates a certain passion."

"Victoria was responsible for that. Even the biographers will tell you this: he was a cold fish—and at best, a reluctant stud. She did all the courting and most of the love-making. Did you know that it was she who proposed to him?"

"I didn't know. Wouldn't that be because she was the monarch of England, and a marriage proposal from him would have been considered incorrect behaviour?"

"That hides the true story, which was quite different."

"What was the true story?"

Carlyle stared out at the carpenters. It was late afternoon and they were ready to quit for the day. One of them was calmly throwing construction debris over the fence into the next yard.

"Even when I met her she was disturbed by the prospect of a life with the man who became Albert, the prince consort. They'd already met by then, and she didn't call him by name—not then, or ever. He was her 'fiance', and later on he was 'the Prince', and when she used either name there was a certain distaste in her tone, as if she were sipping vinegar. It wasn't until long after that first meeting that I understood her."

"Then you saw her again?"

He turned on me. At first he held himself tense, but then his shoulders relaxed and he slumped against the back of the chair.

"Of course. You know I saw her again. Several times that winter in London, and the next summer at Windsor. Each time, she sent a messenger with very precise instructions as to when and where we could safely meet. I followed the instructions...."

There was a long and tentative silence which I, realizing that he had no interest in pursuing this line of questioning, broke first.

"Did you ever speak to her about Albert?"

"She talked about him from those first days, although in the beginning, of course, she couldn't name him. She'd known for some years that he was probably going to be her husband. What she wanted from me were assurances that I didn't care, and that I understood her obligations."

"Did you care?"

"No. Victoria let me know what I meant to her in her own way, and it was something beyond Albert and the meager range of his body and soul. You've been through enough of the documentation to know what I mean by that. It was common knowledge among those close to the royal family that Albert was not interested in Victoria emotionally or sexually. Besides that, I was a married man in my late forties, and a commoner. As a matter of record, I encouraged the marriage because I knew it was inevitable, and later on I encouraged the begetting of the children."

"You encouraged her to have nine children? Why?"

"Don't be a dunce. I encouraged her to have children because I knew her nature, and because the next-in-lines to the Throne were fools, villains or cretins. There was the Empire to consider, ridiculous as that may seem to you. That she had nine of them was accountable to the times and, I suppose, to that nature I spoke of."

"After their marriage?"

"After their marriage what? Did I see her? You know I saw her. I didn't see her very often, and then only at her request."

"Where and how?"

"Different locations. After Osborne House was built—Albert took the opportunity to indulge in his fantasy of being a great architect, which is why the building is a nightmare of Italianesque vulgarity—Victoria convinced him to have a miniature Swiss chalet built for the children. We met there for nearly a decade."

"Did you know Lord Melbourne at all?"

Carlyle swept the air from in front of him with an awkward gesture.

"Blasted air-conditioning," he muttered.

I ignored his self-inflicted distress, and repeated my question.

"I never met Melbourne," he said, distractedly, continuing to paw at the air. "I think he might have been responsible for some of the early attention I got, from people like the critic John Sterling. Victoria cared very deeply for Melbourne, so much so that she never truly forgave Albert for destroying him in 1842. Melbourne, I understand, was an odd man, courtly and cultured, and so confidently English about it that nearly everyone adored him. But for all of that, and perhaps because of it, he could imagine no other world than the one he lived in, and he treated Germans as if they were barbarians. That didn't go down well with any of the Hanovers or their relatives. But whatever one might say of him, he did love Victoria as passionately as anyone ever did. It was never physical, though, if that's what you're thinking. None of Victoria's men were what you would consider passionate men."

"Except you."

"I was different from the others in a variety of ways, yes."

Carlyle sighed; at least he tried to. About halfway into it, the sigh was intercepted by something in his digestive system that might once have been a hiccup or a belch, but was now sheer malevolence. The thing was not so much intent on escaping Carlyle's body as it was on attacking whatever lay beyond its gastric origins. Carlyle tried to stifle it by doubling over. The result was an extrusion of gas so loud it rattled the windows. I froze.

"It's the silent ones you have to worry about," he grunted, still racked by the spasm. "It's an old wives' tale, but it seems to be true."

"Can we talk about the crisis you spoke of earlier?" I asked, leafing quickly back through my notes to find the right one. "Yes. Here it is. You called it a 'fulcrum crisis'. I assume that the fulcrum you referred to is whether the human species is going to go on or whether it's going to blow itself into eternity."

The spasm relaxed, as I'd noted they often seemed to do whenever Carlyle became interested in a topic of conversation.

"The entire human species is involved, but not all of it is up against this crisis. You are, Soviet Russia is, and all the 'white' industrialized world is, in varying degrees. The rest of the world is still engaged in trying to move beyond subsistence. In any event, what you've posed is an existential crisis: well, that's one part of it, but not the whole matter. This crisis cannot be solved simply by patience, or by intellectual pacifism. Indeed, you will need patience, an immense, peaceful patience. But even with that—having made the existential choice to continue, you will still be facing the crisis I spoke about. To get through it, you will require intelligence and ingenuity of a sort you have had little of for half a century."

"You mean since the advent of nuclear weapons?"

"The construction of nuclear weapons is the occasion of the crisis, yes. But mostly symbolically so. Their existence, and the distorted sense of reality they breed, create several peculiar and thoroughly disruptive social phenomena. Most important of these is an absence of purpose amongst those sectors of the population which, in a healthy society, are the conservers of tradition and the arbitrators of value. Those who should be providing positive moral intelligence simply do not believe in a future."

I groaned involuntarily. "That's all incredibly unspecific," I said. "Quite frankly, it's the sort of crap I've heard from government sociologists. I didn't expect to hear it from you. You're asking for leadership and moral density amongst intellectuals. Those things depend on some sort of positive unanimity within the body politic. That doesn't exist any longer, regardless of the presence of nukes. Citizens of good will don't trust anything anymore."

"Do you trust the look in your children's eyes? What do you trust? Apply your blasted pragmatism to something that will afford your children the possibility of a future!"

I recoiled, partly from the vigour of his onslaught, and partly because I heard a suspicious hissing sound as he spoke.

"You look to me for solutions," he said, milder now. "I don't have solutions. I have only language and structure. That's all you can ever look for from the past. Who really knows what is correct or what is 'in error'. That doesn't matter, because it is always going to be confined to insurgence and counter-insurgence unless the way we think is completely altered. You and I have to find some way to reopen ultimate questions; in other words, we have to talk of what is true and what is false."

He turned away from me to look out the window once again. The workmen were leaving, but as they carried their tools out to their truck, the neighbour into whose yard they'd been dumping their construction debris ran out of his house and began to shout at them, so loudly that Carlyle and I could hear him from across the street. Carlyle motioned me to join him at the window.

"I wonder what will happen now?" he said.

The offended neighbour was berating the workmen, two of whom stood, hands on hips and apparently contrite, while the third continued to load tools onto the truck. As we watched, this third workman calmly selected a six-foot length of 2x4 from the truck, walked toward the shouting neighbour, and swung it at his head. The narrow side of the heavy board caught the still shouting man just below the ear, and, not neatly at all, sheared his head off.

Just kidding. Actually, the workman swung the 2x4 in a downward sweep at the neighbour's head but the man ducked aside, and the board came down on his forearm. Carlyle and I simultaneously leaped toward the door to intervene, but by the time we were halfway down the front steps, the second neighbour, the one who had hired the workmen to build the fence, was rushing to the assistance of his downed former antagonist.

"Out!" he hollered to the workmen. "Get yourselves out of here! I hired you to build a fence, not beat up on my neighbours!"

His wife, a severe-looking woman dressed in black latex rubber slacks and halter, followed him down the steps. She was less conciliatory.

"Hit the bastard again," she screamed in a piercingly high voice. "Kick the foreign bastard in the nuts! Pull out his eyeballs!"

Carlyle turned to me. "Is this little pageant supposed to be symbolic?" he asked.

"I don't think so," I said. "But just the same, let's get out of here before it turns into surrealism."

I beat a hasty retreat back to the house, hoping that Carlyle wouldn't ask me about surrealism.

•

He collapsed into a chair, enervated and apparently now uninterested in the scene being played out across the street. He had a habit, I was learning, of lapsing into inattention at precisely the points where D.H. Lawrence would have zoomed forward. Here, Lawrence would have busied himself with trying to trace the mysterious roots of the workman's violence, or with laying down cross-referenced images within the landscape: the wife's latex costumes, the new asphalt pavement, the black vinyl bra pinned across the front of a midnight-blue Camaro parked down the street.

Carlyle, instead, had sunk into a wordless reverie.

"What is it?" I asked.

He looked up into my face with eyes that were hollow with melancholy.

"That woman," he said in a voice that was barely audible. "I just saw Jane."

I put my hand on his shoulder in a gesture of comfort. "I don't know if I understand you." I said.

He shook my hand off. "We fought like that for more than forty years."

"We were talking about a crisis in the human condition," I said, trying to mask some small exasperation and not quite succeeding. "Now you're telling me about your relationship with your wife. I don't get the connection, and I'm sure the reader is going to think something fishy is going on."

He pulled himself from the chair and strode to the window with an almost painful anticipation. The workmen were gone, and my two neighbours were now sitting on the injured one's front porch. The latex-clad wife was folding a sling for the injured arm out of a bedsheet she'd ripped apart. The rest of the sheet—black satin—was in tatters on the lawn.

"I wonder where she got the sheet?" Carlyle mused, slumping against the window-ledge without turning around. The lower half of the window, I noticed, was a lattice of tiny cracks.

"What about your wife?" I asked, trying to steer him in a direction that might clarify his thinking. "I know you didn't get along well, and that both of you wrote a lot of letters back and forth to compensate for the fact that you couldn't stand to be around one another. Was she really such a bitch?"

"By the standards you use, yes. But by those same standards she was also admirable: a fine writer and a feminist-of-sorts. But in our era, domestic life—marriage, sexuality, child-rearing—had the authority of both personal and social necessity, and were not thought of as optional. It seldom occurred to us that we should or could be personally 'fulfilled' by it. We endured it, and usually little more. That's part of your trouble. You are constantly trying to work out your sense of justice in terms of personal gratification. And gratification is the soul of consumer capitalism. In that sense, the so-called radical elements of your society are in agreement with capital in the deepest possible sense."

I was silent. I'd been upset earlier that morning by the thought that I wouldn't be seeing my youngest son because my second ex-wife—his mother—would be taking him to the country for several weeks. Perceiving my distance, Carlyle stared at me righteously for a minute before he went on.

"There are no guaranteed conduits between personal life and the conditions of the body politic. These conduits exist only historically, and as historical self-consciousness fades over the next few decades, perhaps you will be better able to unshackle your minds from wanting the world to love and fondle you."

"Didn't you say that History is over?"

"No. Your thinking implies that, but that is because it is grounded in Marxist historicism. The three-hundred-year process of change I spoke of will have a very different set of consequences, socially, politically, and personally."

I found myself losing focus. Try as I might, it was difficult to imagine a world one hundred and seventy-five years into the future.

"It is possible to live an exemplary life without it being particularly gratifying on a sensual level," he said, as if reading my thoughts. "Your generation can't imagine the future, and so it tends to reject all value that does not lead to quick resolution. You translate questions of value into situationalist existentialism, which is an intellectural procedure that substitutes opportunity for moral value. You self-perpetuate your quandary." He paused. "And will for a little while longer, at least."

•

The prince consort died in 1862. He was not yet fifty: Victoria was forty-three. Thomas Carlyle was sixty-seven years old, and he had not seen Victoria for more than five years at the time. He and the widowed Queen met, discreetly, at Osborne House, four months after Albert's death.

"I'm sorry about Albert," Carlyle said to Victoria, after they'd made love and had settled in amidst the brocaded eiderdown comforters.

"I'm not," the Queen replied. "The bugger died without a struggle. He gave up on me. There was no medical reason for him to die— he simply didn't care enough to go on living."

"Ah."

"Ah, yourself. He spent his entire life demonstrating virtues I cared nothing for. He didn't drink, he rarely smoked, he never ate in excess, and to my knowledge he never relieved himself of bodily wastes. He slept with only one woman in his entire life. He fathered nine children on me, and he fathered each one of them reluctantly. There were times when I wished he had some of his brother's famous vices. Perhaps if he'd had some of those vices, he might have had a few of the skills that my ladies-in-waiting tell me go with them."

"You never once spoke of this."

"I'm the Queen of England. And you knew."

Her imperious persona slipped for an instant and her voice faltered. "Did you know?"

Carlyle shrugged, and in answer, reached into her bodice. The Queen giggled, rolling away from him through the billowing eiderdowns.

They made love again that night, this time without urgency for the first time in many years, and he left her, odalisque, in the tawny summer light of dawn. He left a note on her pillow, but she tore it up after she read it. Sorry.

•

Carlyle woke me up in the middle of the night.

"You wished me to tie all of our discussions to capital," he said, as if interrupting my sleep was a perfectly acceptable and normal thing to do. "I think I have the essentials worked out in a way you might understand."

Still half in a dream, I rolled over and groped along the floor for my glasses. I didn't find them, only the remnants of the starling one of the cats had killed and dragged into the house days before. I sat up and rubbed my eyes. It was a warm early summer night, and through the opened glass doors to the balcony drifted the heavy perfume of honeysuckle. Off in the distance the low hum of traffic was penetrated now and then by the rumble of transport trucks gearing up as they passed over the crest of a nearby hill or gearing down as they climbed it. Outside on the balcony the pelargoniums I'd planted in identical #22 clay pots were in glorious silver-black bloom. Five different varieties of them, and a pot of blue petunias, all monochromatic in the moonlight, were scruffled into fuzz by the absent spectacles.

I stumbled out of bed and took the blue and white cotton samurai robe from its hook on the closet door and threw it across my shoulders.

"Let's sit outside," I said, tying the belt of the robe in a reef-knot around my waist. "The night is still warm. Would you like some coffee?"

"Let's dispense with inessentials," Carlyle said briskly, moving through the doors out onto the balcony and making himself comfortable. "I don't have time to waste. And if you've noticed, I've stoped drinking coffee and tea, thanks to your advanced medical knowledge."

I followed him out onto the balcony, and still half asleep, tried to be chatty about his improved digestion. He cut me short again.

"Capital is a recurrent structural phenomenon across human cultures, not an invention of industrial civilization. Most often it seems to be the manifestation of an inaccurate distribution of wealth."

I snapped wide awake. "That's very Marxian of you," I replied. "I suppose you also believe that once the injustices are corrected Utopia blossoms and the state withers away."

"Don't be daft. I spoke of 'inaccurate' distribution of wealth, not 'inequitable' distribution of material wealth. Capital is a fetish, and wealth is the peculiar material object or objects to which the fetish attaches itself and through which it camouflages its activity and its effects on the body politic. In that sense then, the Marxist understanding of capital is backward. Capital is pathological—an energy in search of mass. It is not the product of mass energy, but the madness of its purest products, consumer goods as talismans and so forth."

"It seems to me that capital more often acts as entropy, causing a cessation of a range of fundamental and constructive human activities."

Carlyle let his head lapse forward into his hands in a gesture of concentration. "That is the eventual character of pathological energy. It devours its host. Always. Darwin knew it but suppressed the information. His father, Erasmus, showed it to him."

"Doesn't pathological energy, rather, supplant its host? For instance, the fault of the Marxist Utopia is that in the practice of those societies organized, however imperfectly, around a Marxist political structure, the state has not shown the slightest hint that it intends to wither away. On the contrary, the state has grown, seeking to supplant the mass of people as the recipient of social and economic wealth. And it succeeds to the extent that it remains invisible to citizens."

"You seem to imply that the 'free world' is somehow different."

"It isn't. The western capitalist states fervently believe that they are different, but the truth is that they are merely the flip side of the same coin. Contemporary capitalism has attacked state institutions, but it has been careful not to question the composition of the state itself, the ultimate purpose of which, universally, is to perpetuate the power of the ruling classes. Both sides, capitalist and communist, will tolerate the state as long as it continues to serve the interests of power. But the perception that has to be habitually renewed is that it is all the same system, based on the same functional building blocks. Capitalism simply regards the system from the top down, Marxism from the bottom up. They're all looking at the same monolith."

"That makes the state wholly evil. If you're saying that, are you willing to take it all the way? I somehow doubt that you'd propose, with the populations we have, that the state can or should wither away."

"No," Carlyle replied without hesitating, "the state won't wither away, and it doesn't have to, although Marx was onto something there. Arbitrary authority and privilege have always been the chief characteristics of the state. What Marx wanted, finally, and before he lost his grip—Trotsky as well—was a condition of social relations in which the state functions solely as a means to enable and support discourse without public violence."

A ray of light penetrated my fog. "You're repeating what you said earlier about the first priority of a democratic state being to provide conceptual equipment to its citizens; education, in other words."

"That's not exactly the way I would have put it," Carlyle smiled, "but it will do. The French Revolution failed because it mistook its mandate. When Charlotte Corday approached Marat and demanded that the revolution guarantee her happiness—and Marat agreed to guarantee it—the Revolution was doomed. The state is something that must be re-thought and then rebuilt by each generation. Any state that does not visibly concentrate on providing its citizens with the tools to carry out that reconstruction is actively attempting to prevent change. And if this sounds terribly idealistic to you, think about the conditions you live under, in which all the massive wealth of your time is aimed at guaranteeing and protecting ignorance of the many, fostering misinformation and half-truth. Consider it!"

•

Carlyle was back at his post in front of the window, this time gazing at the exquisite lattice of cracks along its lower edge.

"How was this done?" he asked, vaguely.

I shrugged. "They're old windows," I lied. "There's no telling how or why this happened. Glass is a liquid, actually, like water, except that it runs more slowly. So if one were to build a glass house against the winds of change, sooner or later, without the throwing of a single stone, it would cease to exist because the panes of glass would simply run out the bottom of the window frames."

"You're referring to the Crystal Palace?"

"Not really. I'm trying to explain the distortions in that window you're looking at."

"This window is shattered in an interesting way," he replied cuttingly. "And you've been covering me in cliches. Stop it."

He turned back to the window without waiting for my answer. Across the street I could see, distorted by the irregular thickness of the window glass, the houses of my neighbours and the top of the barren fence that separated their properties. Both houses seemed deserted; the windows shut, the drapes pulled. I sensed something was ending, and wondered idly if either neighbour knew that the glass in their windows was slowly but inexorably sliding downward and would eventually form a small mound of clear silicon at the base of each window frame.

"What language did you and Victoria speak while you were together," I asked Carlyle, who'd been lulled, or bored, into a state of somnabulance by my meditation on the nature of glass.

He blushed visibly. "Uh, German. Almost always. She admired my translations of Goethe, and since both of us spoke it fluently, we used it. She wrote...."

He stopped abruptly and sat down.

"She wrote what?" I prompted.

"Nothing." His voice suddenly closed on itself. "A few poems. Not very good ones. The diary you already know about."

"I didn't intend to give up that secret," I replied.

"I thought you wanted to alter the procedures of story-writing. If you withhold a source of information, then it seems to me that you continue to support all the current illusions about the power and authority of the narrator in stories."

"Well, I do want to change that," I replied, feeling a little confused. "But I also want to be loyal to my sources of information."

"Then why did you ask if we spoke German?"

"Because the diary is written in English."

"So were the diaries that are known to exist. Why should this one be in another language."

Editor's Note: The diary referred to is one of four written diaries the author found in the attic of the Manor House, Rushlake Green, Heathfield, Sussex, England, in December 1962. The writer of one of the diaries names herself, variously, "Victoria" and "Eliza" within its pages. The diary carries no signature. The writer of two of the other diaries signs himself "Thos Carlyle of Chelsea, London" in both books. The fourth diary is in German and remains untranslated to date. The author has disclosed the existence of these diaries with some reluctance and without explanation.

"Just a hunch. I suspected that the relationship was conducted in German, and I was puzzled by the diary being in English. Keeping the diary in German would have been a hedge against discovery."

"Ridiculous deduction!" Carlyle exploded. "Everyone in the royal household spoke and read German. What are you trying to say —that the diary is not authentic? If that's true, what am I doing here, and why are we talking?"

"What do you take me for?" I answered, equally incensed.

"Well, what do you take me for," Carlyle replied. "Do you think I'm only in this for the gossip? That isn't all there is to a story."

"I know, I know," I replied, apologetic. "I know that better than most."

•

"What happened after Jane died?" I asked Carlyle not long after our somewhat acrimonious exchange concerning the diary.

"That was 1866," he answered, and then paused, darkening visibly. "Difficult days for both of us."

"Both of whom?" I asked.

Carlyle ignored the obvious jibe.

"When I met Jane," he said, "she was a great beauty. And a beauty of great intelligence and some sweetness."

"What went wrong?"

"What always goes wrong. We are not what we seem. Never. Jane craved a father figure: one with a foundation of stone, admitting of no weakness. I was not, despite appearances, made of stone." Carlyle suddenly giggled like a schoolgirl. "She couldn't bear my lack of a beard."

"You're jesting."

"Not at all, and stop trying to speak like I do or I'll revert to the German syntax for which I'm famous. One reason why we got along so well when we were apart was that she kept a photograph of me on her writing table. Thus, and only thus, could she believe in me. And in my stony discourse. But even that she couldn't believe in when I was physically present. She wanted me to be made of stone, which as you can see, I'm not."

I could see that, for reasons of his own, he wasn't prepared to be serious about his wife, so I moved on.

"When Jane died, what did Victoria do?"

"For a little while she did nothing. You've seen the letter she finally wrote to me in the public archive: April 1866. Several days after that, no more than a week, I received word by messenger to meet her at a manor house in Sussex."

"Rushlake Green."

"Yes. That's where you found her diary. She brought it whenever and wherever we met—for me to read aloud in the night. As I grew older, you know, I ceased to sleep—particularly around her. Each hour seemed too valuable to squander in dream."

"And you had an audience several years later?"

Carlyle twisted in his chair, as if the reminder drove a cramp into his slowly unwinding intestines.

"Ah," he said, his voice as quiet as the wind. "Ah, yes. That. We spoke across a room then. And as if it made real to her the gulf that truly had always existed between us, that public meeting ended everything between us."

"You'd seen her recently? The night before?"

"You have no information on that," Carlyle answered sternly. "You're guessing. Or hoping. And you should know the difference between an informed guess and an ignorant one."

"Then this is the end," I said.

"Unless we go over it again," he said, matter-of-factly. "You know, when I look all this over, I have to admit that your alternatives are rather uninviting. You can tie the elements into a neat narrative bundle and provide an entirely arbitrary ending, thereby putting the story back into the nineteenth century. Or you can cease here, at the limits of what you can credibly know, in which case you will annoy and alienate many of your possible readers."

I had to admit that my prospects didn't look good, so I did. "Just two questions more," I added. "Let me tie in two last strands."

Carlyle pulled himself from the chair, and, fighting off yet another disquisition within his innards, smiled wanly at me.

"You must do what you must. But they're your questions entirely, so beware of the answers, or at least of how you handle them."

"Okay," I said, impatiently brushing aside his qualifier. "First question: what about the crabs?"

"I had no crabs. And I can truthfully tell you I know nothing of Victoria's. What have you got written on that sheet of foolscap over there?" he said, walking quickly to the table and picking up a sheet of yellow foolscap I hadn't seen until that moment.

He handed it to me without looking at it. I looked at it for a long time without understanding the words, written across it in green ink by a neat hand.

"It isn't my handwriting," I said dubiously, and then read the words aloud:

"Buckingham Palace, November 1887. In a major breach of palace procedures and in an act that, if detected, would have brought instant dismissal, an upstairs Lady of Chamber, one Alice Merton, formerly of Ipswich, used the Queen's personal facilities to effect one of the more specialized and private of female toiletries. She had been, for some days previous, in a state of considerable discomfort due to an itch contracted by unknown means. She was then seventeen years of age, and a virgin. She died in a Stepney hostel four days after the death of Queen Victoria in 1901, of causes unknown."

I looked up at Carlyle as I finished reading. He shrugged, but made no comment.

"What's your second question," he said, at length.

"A tougher one," I replied. "I'm not sure how one might answer it."

"State the question."

"Well. I'm dissatisfied with my explanation of your relationship to D.H. Lawrence. It's too arbitrary. Where does he come from, and where does he fit?"

"He doesn't fit," Carlyle said, after a moment's thought. "At least not in any conventional way. He appeared because he believed in the reality of the imagination—both of images and of the generative landscapes poetry provides for thought. What you and I have shared here, and in our lives, is an uneasiness with those things. That uneasiness has been manifested, at different times, from every position possible—by both radical disbelief and sentimental longing, and from every position in between."

"So what's the right one?"

"Don't be pedantic," Carlyle chided. "That's another annoying characteristic we share. You don't know. I don't know. Some things are not known. In some ways this story has already been told."

TALONBOOKS— FICTION IN PRINT 1984

Songs My Mother Taught Me—Audrey Thomas
Blown Figures—Audrey Thomas
Hungry Hills—George Ryga
Theme for Diverse Instruments—Jane Rule
Mrs. Blood—Audrey Thomas
Night Desk—George Ryga
Ballad of a Stonepicker—George Ryga
Durer's Angel—Marie Claire Blais
A Short Sad Book—George Bowering
Desert of the Heart—Jane Rule
The Woman Who Got On at Jasper Station & Other Stories—Howard O'Hagan
Wilderness Men—Howard O'Hagan
Latakia—Audrey Thomas
The Con Man—Ken Mitchell
Prisoner of Desire—britt hagarty
The Fat Woman Next Door Is Pregnant—Michel Tremblay
Real Mothers—Audrey Thomas
Sad Paradise—britt hagarty
My Career with the Leafs & Other Stories—Brian Fawcett
Chameleon & Other Stories—Bill Schermbrucker
The Circus Performers' Bar—David Arnason
Capital Tales—Brian Fawcett